GRIMBEARD

Tales of the Last Dwarf

Written and Illustrated by
Samwise Didier

INSIGHT 👁 EDITIONS

San Rafael, California

INSIGHT
EDITIONS

PO Box 3088
San Rafael, CA 94912
www.insighteditions.com

f Find us on Facebook: www.facebook.com/InsightEditions
🐦 Follow us on Twitter: @insighteditions

Library of Congress Cataloging-in-Publication Data available.

ISBN: 978-1-60887-919-9

PUBLISHER: Raoul Goff
ART DIRECTOR: Chrissy Kwasnik
EXECUTIVE EDITOR: Vanessa Lopez
PRODUCTION EDITORIAL MANAGER: Alan Kaplan
PROJECT EDITORS: Greg Solano and Mark Irwin
PRODUCTION EDITOR: Elaine Ou
PRODUCTION MANAGER: Alix Nicholaeff
BOOK LAYOUT: Amy DeGrote

ROOTS of PEACE   🌿 REPLANTED PAPER

Insight Editions, in association with Roots of Peace, will plant two trees
for each tree used in the manufacturing of this book. Roots of Peace is
an internationally renowned humanitarian organization dedicated to
eradicating land mines worldwide and converting war-torn lands into
productive farms and wildlife habitats. Roots of Peace will plant two
million fruit and nut trees in Afghanistan and provide farmers there
with the skills and support necessary
for sustainable land use.

Manufactured in China by Insight Editions

10 9 8 7 6 5 4 3 2 1

Dedicated to everyone who knows
dwarves are way cooler than elves.

CONTENTS

GRIMBEARD
GOES TO PRISON

THE CREW
Prison Bound

Legends will tell the story soon enough, I guess, but until then I'll just have to spoil it and say, with all humility and unpretentiousness, that I am the best damn captain who ever sailed these or any other seas. But I can only take about a quarter of the credit, see. As anyone will tell ya, a captain is only as good as his crew, his cook, and his ship. And this tale will tell ya how I got the hat trick on all of it!

So the workday was over and I started going over the spoils from my latest conquest. I took a few elfin merchant drone ships by surprise and managed to board them without incident. The booty was nothing worth getting excited over, though. A few hundred pounds of elfin silks, some new techno-devices the elfs hawk called ePhones, and a bunch of crates packed full of mo-mos, a sticky, sweet elfin fruit that whenever I eats it, makes me chum the waters from both ends.

Anyways, I was sailing, pondering my situation, and I started chatting with the *Ol' Girl*, my ship. Now, to make it clear, this isn't the *new Ol' Girl*—you know, the one that is all flying around, magically bound in the bones of a big old dragon. No, this is the *old Ol' Girl*, before her new refurbishments. So she and I were puttering around the Azurewine Ocean, and I said, "Ya know, girl, I think I might be needing to take on a crew again."

The *Ol' Girl* just sailed on and listened quietly (she's always been good like that), and I continued on with my lamentations.

"It's not that we can't do this stuff ourselves; we've raided some small elf vessels and suffered through enough typhoons and nasty croctopusses to last a while. But this next leg of our journey might require more than just my two mitts and your cannons, you know? I aims to take on the entire elfin military and pays them back for what they done to my kin."

Now in case you don't know what in Bor's bloody beard I am talking about, I'll brief ya. A couple hundred years ago (give or take a few more centuries), the elfs and dwarfs, once bitter enemies, put aside their differences and teamed up against the greatest monsters of the day: trolls, dragons, beastlings, and giants, all those types of villainous scoundrels.

The dwarfs, what with our mastery of stonework and engineering, were in charge of constructing the big old prisons called Omega-Maxes to hold these cretins.

The elfs were responsible for rustling up all the beasties and bringing them in. No short work on either side: the elfs rounded them up, and the dwarfs socked them away.

So when the work was done and the realm was free of the monstrosities, the elfs turned traitorous on me and my kin and wiped out the entire dwarf civilization! Well, through circumstances beyond my control, I managed to escape the whole "getting genocided" thing because I was at a . . . I'm sorry; here I am, rambling away, when this story is about how I got my crew. I'll save that ol' dwarven genocide tale for another time.

So, as I was saying to the *Ol' Girl,* "Not only do I needs a crew, but I needs a crew with some muscle to back my plans to overthrow them pointy-eared, moth-winged runts and—" Oh, you didn't know elfs had wings? Yes sir, they love fluttering around, leaving sparkly elfy dust everywhere. I'll talks more about them later, so just be patient now.

I broke out an old map of all the islands the prisons was located on, and I started to plot our course. I figured if I could bust open the prisons, then I'd have a veritable army of monsters on my side. All I had to do was convince thousands of ornery prisoners—at least them that are still living—that I was sorry for locking them up for all those years, and offer them restitution by allowing them to crush their hated enemies, the elfs. I mean, who ain't itching to smash some pretentious elf dogs? Well, I actually likes dogs. How about pretentious elf cats?

Now, over the next few weeks, the *Ol' Girl* and I sailed on through hurricanes and battle croctopusses . . . or is it croctopi? Mmm, pie. I bet a baked croctopus pie would be fantastic! Well, I'm getting off track again, and I ain't got no master chef to cook them pies anyway, so let's get back to the story.

So I searches the various prisons we bump into, and I ain't expecting much, 'cause it has been a thousand years since I first locked them rascals away. Unfortunately, I guess the elfs had a map of the prison locations as well, and from the looks of it, they found them a few hundred years before I did. Every Omega-Max was in some state of ruination. The walls were blown apart by elfin laz cannons, and the areas around them were blackened and scorched by thermal melta-bombs. Heh, not the standard bow-and-sorcery elfs from the old days; these boys pack some serious destructive firepower now. Guess they didn't want to risk the chance of a prison break, and they just blasted them from the skies. Lucky for the monsters, elfs is terrible shots. I bet most of the prisoners got away to start the whole monster circle of life again. Ah well.

Me and the *Ol' Girl* scouted a few more prisons, but all were the exact same, full of devastation and sunken hopes of finding me an army and a crew. I was starting to get into one of my moods when I saw something on my map that I had completely forgot about. It was an island marked with a question mark, and it had a bunch of squiggly arrows pointing all around the surrounding area. That's right! The Mega-Omega-Max prison! This one (I just call her M.O.M.) was made to house the most vilest of the vile and keep them locked up in her stony bosom forever.

M.O.M. is a magical creation, a completely automated prison that floats around the seas so nobody can ever locate it. It is powered by

magic runes, and it even has an automated galley, water wells, and stone golems to police it. It boasts a great rec yard, and in some areas, it has crystal scrying spheres (aka crystal balls) that show you what's going on in the outside world, kind of like the plasma screens you see around in these current future-istical days. Yeah, M.O.M. was a marvel indeed—some of my finest work, if I do say so myself.

Oh, you look surprised. That's right: *my* work. I know it is hard to believe, but, besides being the best damn captain these waters has ever seen, I am a damn fine runesmith to boot! Runesmith, you say? Yep, runesmith. See, just about any dwarf worth his stones could make a simple penitentiary out of rock, but when you want something a bit more exceptional, you goes to a runesmith.

I don't recall much about my youth, just a lot of jumbled memories and the like. But learning runesmithing, I remember. It was taught to me by my grandpappy, who went by the name of One Eye. At night, my grandpappy and I would steal out on his ol' rowing boat, and by moonlight he would teach me how to carve the bones of magic. Runes can be made of anything—clay, stone, wood—but if you want the most powerful runes, they need to be carved out of the bones of magical creatures—dragons being the preferred, since they are essentially magic incarnate. I don't get dragons, though. For all that magic hoopla, dragons is dumb as lizards, not like those brainy ones in those elfy romance stories you can read on those newfangled ePods they market everywhere. Nope, just big dumb galoots with tails.

Sorry, I got sidetracked. I never really liked dragons.

So some might ask, "Grim, if the prison was made so as not to be found, how did you find it?"

Well, I'll tell ya. See, it was easy for me to find 'cause I gots me all sorts of contraptions and inventions that I made over the years, and one of them is a runic compass. Yep, it can detect the presence of runic magic and point me in the general direction. So I dug through my beard and pulled it out (after some difficulty), and me and the *Ol' Girl* started sailing toward the appointed area. After a few days of maelstroms and croctopus battles, we spots ol' M.O.M. dead ahead. I ties off the *Ol' Girl* to one of the docks and strolls up toward the main gate, fumbling around in my beard for the gate key. I jams the key in, and after I used some fancy elbow grease I had on hand, the mechanisms turned and the gates opened for the first time in a thousand years.

I remembers the last time I was at these gates, there was this little runt, a couple of feet taller than me, who broke free from his skinny elf- ish captors' restraints and charged me. Well, reacting with my normal greasy-slick reflexes, I clocked him so hard I busted off one of the big goofy horns he had on his helmet. The stone golems led him off, him cursing me all the while, and the doors shut.

I was walking through the old hallways, reacquainting myself with the layout, when I walked through the main hall and looked into one of those fancy scrying devices. In the sphere, I should be looking at cells of inmates locked up for eternity, but all I saw was a bunch of empty rooms.

Bor's bloody beard, what was going on in here? Where were all my soon-to-be crewmembers? And where were the sentries? They're miss- ing too! I figured I'll go check the rec yard, and guess what I saw? The whole yard was swarming with prisoners—beastlings, trolls, and the like—all hanging out, eating, and brawling without one guard in sight. I looked in the center of the yard and saw this humongous-looking char- acter dressed in black plate mail, shouting above the fracas.

"Bjorn Huge crave drink. Bjorn Huge want more plop!"

I nearly forgot about plop! Plop is the food source M.O.M. makes to keep the inmates fed. See, the island is automated to house and feed all the miscreants, and plop is a high-protein, high-fiber, calorically dense food source that the prison makes to nourish them. Basically, beneath

M.O.M. is a series of large nets that drag the waters underneath her, dredging up anything it can. Seaweed, slugs, shells, and other such delectable items get scooped up and dumped into M.O.M.'s steam cookers, which break down all the components into a speckled pink and gray, translucent paste. I was just remembering how awful plop tasted when I heard a triumphant roar.

"YOUUUU!" screamed the big armored cuss in the yard.

He stood up, shaking off his cloak to reveal a massively muscled torso and a set of legs that looked thick as the *Ol' Girl*'s mast!

Wow, he would be a great addition to my new crew, I thought wistfully. I said I needed some muscle, and this guy was loaded with it! I jumped down into the yard and stalked up to him like I owned the joint, 'cause, in reality, I did. A few of his lackeys got in my way and found out that there ain't any soft spots on my fists. I walked up to him and offered my hand.

"Grimbeard's the name, *Captain* Grimbeard to the likes of you, big boy," I said with all my manners.

He loomed in all close like, and his big shadow fell over me like a heavy, wet tarp.

"I have longed for this day, vile dwarf! Do you not remember Bjorn Huge?" he said, all malevolently.

I must admit that someone of his stature would be hard to forget. He was a good ten feet tall and encased in black and gold plate mail.

I ♡ M.O.M

He looked magnificent in his regalia, until my eyes fell on the helm he had covering his gigantic melon. Now normally this thing would have been the piece that ties up the whole "I'm a bad dude; don't mess with me" vibe ol' Bjorny was trying to achieve. He would've done it, too, if it weren't for one thing: his big old helmet was missing a horn on one side. I chuckled, finally remembering who he was.

"Ahh, it's you! Boy-o, you've gotten big! Who'd have thought plop could produce such fantastic results?"

"Bahhh, Bjorn Huge grew all by himself! I grew strong by battling others trapped in cage. When I defeat all the rest, I defeat stupid guards as well. See the trophies I wear upon my armor! Bjorn is chieftain of Monster Island!"

Now I didn't like the idea of this brute calling M.O.M., the magical engineering wonder I lovingly created, something as lowbrow as "Monster Island," but what got me steamed was the trophies he collected. I didn't pay no attention to the horns and scalps dangling from his frame; it was the *runes of life* stuck to his armor that got me fuming. See, each of the sentries that guarded M.O.M. was a stone construct affectionately made by yours truly, and each one bore a rune of life, a magical sigil that, when attached to an inanimate object, breathes life to the lifeless. Each golem had one attached to its helmet. Now those runes were hammered irreverently to ol' Bjorn's armor like some carnival trinkets, and that got me mad. I tried to placate myself; I needed to keep my manners in, as I was trying to win over the old bucket head to my cause.

"Now those are some fantastic trophies you got there, Bjorny. How would you like to join my crew? I believe someone of your apparent hugeness would be useful to my cause," I said with the sweetness of a pint of honey.

Bjorn put his hands on his hips and laughed arrogantly.

"Bjorn Huge is king here, little dwarfling. I serve under no one except Bjorn Huge! Now it time for me to pay you back for damage you did to mighty helm so many years ago." Bjorn Huge reached back and pulled out an axe from somewhere.

I looked around at the lackeys to make sure they was behaving themselves and not trying to sneak up on me. Then I offered up a deal.

"How about this? If I defeat you in honorable combat, you and your guys will be my crew and help me fight the elfs. If I loses, you can have the key to this joint, and you can sail away to freedom on my ship. Deal?" I asked, holding out my hand.

"Deal," he said, and just as I was about to shake on it, he swung his axe and slammed it down. Fortunately for me, I been fighting these giant types all my life, and my quickness of foots saved my beard from getting parted from my chin. The big axe lodged into the wall, sticking itself in nicely. Bjorn abandoned the axe and picked up something a bit duller: a troll. He hurled the poor thing at me and knocked me into a pen of dire wolf puppies. They scampered away, with everyone trying to grab them so they wouldn't get squashed in the squabble.

Seeing me sprawled amongst the wolf turds, Bjorn started getting his chest all puffed out, thinking he had himself a new boat and freedom. The sun was shining behind him, and his dang shadow started falling on me all menacing-like. If I didn't do something, I wouldn't be needing a crew anymore; I'd need pallbearers. I spied an ol' copper dog bowl that held the funkiest-looking bone I ever seen before, three feet's worth of green, gnawed, and gnarly. I grabbed the bowl and held it toward the sun peeking behind ol' Bjorny. With an expert eye and a bit of dwarven luck, I caught the sun and reflected it right in between the plates of his goofy-looking helmet. Bjorn cried and whipped back his bucket head. Without wasting a second, I winged the copper bowl and smacked him in his dome. His helmet rang like a bell, and he started windmilling backwards, slipping in the wolf pee and stumbling over his men. I didn't think it was going to do anything except buy me some precious seconds, but it turned out slightly different than I intended.

Bjorn fell back against the wall—yep, the one where his axe was buried. He landed on that axe and, in one fell swoop, managed to claim another trophy for his collection: his own head. His body went stumbling around the yard, and all the while his head kept yelling for it to get back and pick him up. It was kind of disturbing, as it went on for a while.

"See, dwarf, you can't defeat Bjorn Huge! I will crush you!" his helmet shouted, and I tell you the truth here that his dang head started hopping around after me. He managed to get a good couple of head-butts in before I could rassle him down. I ended up sitting on the helmet, but damned if I didn't get bucked off a time or two. I looked down and saw one of those runes of life I had carved so many years ago, all nailed to his helmet. If these runes are so powerful they can animate two tons of stone statue to life, I guess one of them can keep an overly large head kicking about. Ah, I wish I could tell my grandpappy. He would have laughed!

Anyway, Bjorn started getting all uppity, and I began to lose my manners.

"Game over, Bjorny. You lost! Now, either you ship up or head out."

Yeah, I knows that was rather mean to say to the disembodied head I was sitting on, but I was getting into one of my moods.

"But I still live. Bjorn Huge still rule Monster Island!"

He kicked into fussy mode, trying to gore me with his one remaining horn. Finally I got really fruster-ated, and with one booted foot, I sent him flying across the yard, where he landed in a sewage drain. As he fell into the drain, he kept yelling that "it's a tie" and that "Bjorn Huge did not die!" After a few clangs of him bouncing around the pipes, I heard him yell something about losing his horn, and then I heard a big wet splash, and that was it for the mighty Bjorn Huge.

Needless to say, the rest of the villains didn't put up no fight, eager to leave the island and get some fresh salt air into their lungs. Unfortunately, my mission had only started. I still had another couple of stops before we would ship off of M.O.M. The monsters started grumbling, but I silenced them with a bark. I got hands now, but with the loss of old Bjorny, I'd need someone with some muscle to keep these dogs in line. I took out my trusty map, and upon further perusal, I located my next prize.

"All right, crew. I am off to get our star player, Mon'Goro, the dreaded warlord of the wastes and—"

For some reason, my new crew erupted into a cannonade of guffaws and cackles. I started fuming, and two or three of the comedians went to sleep due to two or three fist kisses.

A grimy-looking crossbreed named Gruesome politely raised his hand (remember your manners, kids) and told me that Mon'Goro had changed a bit over the years and that I would find him in M.O.M.'s galley.

"What does the warlord of the wastes find himself doing in my galley?" I asked, all bewilderedly. I started looking around for some sort of weapon. Normally my wits and my fists are all I needs, but against madman Mon'Goro, I wanted some backup.

My crew started chuckling again, and once more a few suffered the effects of fist-induced narcolepsy. Gruesome held his hands up and patted my shoulders in a friendly manner.

"Just go to the galley, Captain," said Gruesome. "All will become clear."

You know, now that I thinks about it, I likes Gruesome. I wonders whatever happened to him.

That's it for this chapter, youngsters. Stay tuned for when I stands up against the warlord of the wastes himself!

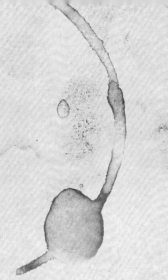

THE CHEF
Snap, Crackle, and Plop Tarts

I was getting plumb tired of dealing with these scallywags (aka my crew) already, and it hadn't even been ten minutes yet. I desperately needed someone that could wrangle these goons into a squad of maulers. You know, a model individual that they could aspire to be, one of their own. That's why I needed Mon'Goro. In the old days, he led the largest war parties ever known to dwarf- or elfkind. He sacked gleaming elfin cities and raided the iron mines of the dwarves too many times to count. He was a real son of a beastling!

My thoughts were suddenly interrupted by the most awful sound these old ears ever heard before. It sounded something like a choir of alley cats that was in heat, all meowing at the moon. After going through this ear torture, I realized it was only the sound of an elf organ playing at top volume. I hustled toward the galley and was greeted by a truly horrific sight. But then the smell hit me, and all of a sudden the sight wasn't as frightful.

I walked into the galley, and it looked like a laboratory of some mad, demented chef! Helmets was being used as cooking pots; old shields was hammered flat into what resembled griddles. The organ sounds was coming out of a bunch of those crystal ball thingies I mentioned to you earlier. Every one of the magic spheres were showing images of a bunch of fluffy clouds, and all the while some deep voice—well, deep for an elf, that is—droned on theatric-ally.

"*As the sands of time slip through our grasp, so do-eth our days turn-eth into night.*"

"Bor's moldy mustache, why is a bloody soap opera playing in my galley?!"

I felt a prickling of my neck hairs, and a gravely baritone whisper crept up behind me:

"Not a soap opera, friend, but one of the finest pieces of elfin culture we are privileged to see. Stories of honor, courage, love, and sorrow, an artistic mélange skillfully edited into hour-long episodes, minus commercials."

I wheeled around, cursing myself for getting crept up on. Only somebody with the stealth of a bloody shadow panther could get the drop on me, and that somebody just so happened to be the person I was looking for. I pulled out my friendliest voice and started my pitch.

"Now listen up, you dirty scallywag of a—" I was cut short by what I saw. I had expected to see the dreaded warlord of the wastes, all eight feet and five hundred pounds of purple snarling ferocity, standing behind me. Instead what I saw was just a fart in that general area of ferocity. He was tall enough, but those five hundred pounds looked to have jumped up a few hundred pounds, and instead of rusty red chain mail, he was sporting a ratty old apron. The most awful thing, though, was the snarl. Well, if it was a snarl, it would have been frightening, and I could have dealt with frightening. What I couldn't handle was what was in the snarl's place. It looked like a big, toothy, fang-filled smile.

"Welcome to my humble quarters, little one. May I offer you some refreshments? I have a batch of plop tarts baking right now."

The grape-hued mountain moved over toward a stack of breastplates that had been hammered together into a crude-looking oven. He popped it open and wolfed down a few tarts, shaking his head.

"Two minutes," he said, closing up the "oven" before turning back to me. "Now, what is it that I can help you with?" Just then, the organ music ended and another tune started. This one was upbeat and accompanied by crowds cheering.

"Please excuse me. My favorite show, *Staaaart Cooking*, is on. I never miss it." He hurried over to a bunch of mattresses he had laid on the ground like floor mats and sat down gracefully upon them. About fifteen crystal balls blared out the cooking show.

"Please, take off your boots and pull up a mattress! The contestants are making mo-mo noodles today. I have extra plop-corn, if you like. Sorry, no butter, though; it is bad for the heart."

I was dumbfounded. Here I was, being entertained by the baddest (well, once the baddest), most ruthless beastling that walked this here world, and now he was concerned about my heart? He used to collect hearts on spears, and now he wouldn't even let me put butter on my plop-corn? I walked between the crystal balls and Mon'Goro, blocking them from his vision, and started my pitch again.

"I don't rightly know what's come over you, but the Mon'Goro I remember was a reaver, a slayer! And that is just the villain I needs to lead my crew. I'm looking to go to battle with the elfs, and I needs the warlord of the wastes at my side! What do you say?"

Grimbeard Goes to Prison

His answer was as lightning quick as his reflexes.

"No, thank you," he said all seriously.

I riposted with my own quickness.

"Come on . . . glory, booze, elf women, you know, all the stuff a warlord of your likes needs."

"Vanity, bad for liver, too thin for my tastes," he deftly blocked, parried, and countered.

He stood up, and I was expecting him to get in my beard and start having it out with me, but instead, he just walked over to the oven again and opened it with a big old grin.

"The tarts are ready," he said proudly.

"I don't get it," I said loudly. "Here I am, promising you freedom and spoils and battle, and all you are worrying about is your bloody plop tarts! You used to be the terror of the realm, and now you act like nothing but a bloody . . . a bloody elfin chef!"

That seemed to get a reaction out of him. His eyes got all big and round, and his jaw dropped. He flew over to me so fast I barely had time to throw my arms up and block the inevitable flurry of fists that was to follow. Instead of beating me, he wrapped me in his arms and started squeezing me. Then, if you can believe it, I heard a sobbing sound and felt the wet slick of tears on my beard! I shook free and fell to the ground unceremoniously, and Mon'Goro helped me up.

"Thank you, thank you, kind dwarf. Your words have made all the hard work over these past hundreds of years worth it. To compare my tarts to those of an elfin chef, it means so much—" And he started blubbering again.

I forgot to mention that I didn't mean it as a compliment in the first place. Geez, I never even tried his plop tarts! I helped him compose himself and allowed him to keep the handkerchief I offered him when he filled it to capacity. After he settled down, I sat cross-legged next to him on his mat (after, of course, I removed my boots).

I continued my verbal castigations. "What in Bor's blazing beard happened to you, Mongo?"

He sat there with the tray of plop tarts in his hand, lost in his thoughts. Then the drama department unleashed its new play.

"When I was brought to this prison, my soul was furious! My arrogance couldn't conceive that I, Mon'Goro, had been captured. Caged like a beast! The warlord of the wastes was nothing more than a kept dog. For years I consoled myself with wanton violence and slaughter, trying to abate the pain of my ignominious incarceration."

I closed my eyes and waved him on, trying to hurry up this new soap opera I was being forced to watch with no commercial interruptions.

"The destruction I wrought caused only more pain and turmoil. I sought out the greatest champions of the prison yards and defeated them soundly in duels to the death. I defeated them all without effort. Without the challenge of battle, I became withdrawn. I gave up the yard to an arrogant young upstart with a silly helmet, and I wandered the halls of the prison, alone and hopeless. That is, until I was saved."

Oh boy, here it comes, I thought, getting ready to defend myself against some newfangled religion he must've gotten. I don't stomach religions in general. You can have 'em; just keep them out of my galley. Turns out it wasn't religion that saved him, but it sure was something just as silly.

"What saved me," he continued reverently, "was something as simple as what you see in this platter."

I looked down, and there was nothing but crumbs on his empty cooking sheet. He saw this and proceeded to take the last half-chewed plop tart out of his mouth and place it in the tray.

"Huh?" I mumbled like a fool. I had no idea what this guy was getting at until he pointed to the crystal balls and showed me the light.

On-screen, a bunch of elfs was running around a kitchen, grabbing dishes of this and bottles of that. It looked like they was competing or something, as another elf counted down and finally squealed, "Stooooop cooking!"

Mon'Goro was totally enthralled. The elf announcer gleefully declared to a spastic elf that he was the winner. The audience clapped, Mon'Goro clapped, and I slapped myself for watching this crap.

"So let me get this straight. You were the greatest warrior this realm ever saw, and a cooking show—"

"This chef d'oeuvre is not just a cooking show. It showed me a new way of life!" After he explained to me that the funky "chez-doover" word means "a masterpiece in literature or art," he continued.

"I learned I could create rather than destroy. I could fill the belly rather than disembowel it."

I jumped in as he popped in the last half of the tart. "And you got all that from that chez-doover cooking show?" I'm naturally good with linguisticals.

He just looked back at me and smiled, as some kind of buzzer went off in the background. He bent down to the oven and came up with a gray brick of steaming baked plop.

"Care for a piece of plop-pernickel?"

I had to think quickly.

"Uh, no, I'm still all full up from all the plop turds—uhh, plop tarts I never ate."

He went about spreading some nasty-looking plop jam on his nasty plop brick whiles I scratched my head in contemplation.

I needed this guy to add some muscle to my new crew, but he weren't no good to me all domesticated and housebroken like this. What I needed to do was get him away from his elfy cooking shows and soap operas. I formulated an idea that I thought might do the trick. I smiled like I cared.

"You ever wish to stretch your culinary muscles with something besides, you know, plop?"

He looked around the galley wistfully. "I do crave the challenge. The cooking shows have new ingredients every week. I have mastered plop over the past hundred years, and besides being so calorically dense, it can also be so limiting. It seems for my remaining years I am doomed to be nothing more than a one-ingredient wonder."

The line I cast had been nibbled on, but I needed to bring out the fat juicy worms if I was gonna land this whale. The figurative whale; I'm not calling Mon'Goro fat. (Well, he could slow down on the plop tarts.)

So I cleared my throat all casually and cast my line again.

"Say, Mon'Goro, what was that absolutely fabulous dish that elf made to win that show there?" I says with all politeness.

Mon'Goro's eyes widen.

"Ohhh, the winner made an undeniably fabulous noodle dish with mo-mos."

"Mo-mos, you say? The super sweet fruit? Well, that is just a shame," I said all dejected-like.

Mon'Goro's face grew worried at my distress.

"What is it you grieve about?" he said, all concerned.

"Well, see, I've found myself looking for someone to head up my crew—uhh, my galley. And believe it or not, I got me a few crates of mo-mos not three hundred yards from where we is standing right now! Unfortunately, they are starting to turn brown and soft, and . . . Well, you don't want to hear none of my sad stories."

Mon'Goro's eyes started to soften, and I saw the drool hanging from his lip as well. I had him now, and all I needed to do was reel him in.

"I guess I'm just going to have to throws them out since, well, I ain't no chef, and you declined my polite offer to join—"

"Enough," spoke Mon'Goro in the voice that had once commanded thousands of beastlings in battle. He walked up to me and looked deep into my eyes. The glare was fiercely intense, and I thought maybe he recognized my ploy, but then I realized I just landed my prize fishy.

"Please, forgive me for refusing your generous offer earlier. You have paid me the highest compliment one could pay in my craft, and while I cannot shed blood for you, I can cook for you and your crew. Besides, I did not know about this dire mo-mo situation that is upon you. I, Mon'Goro, will lead your galley, and together we will save the beloved mo-mos from their destruction."

Boom! That's a wrap for Chapter Two.

THE DRAGON
Roll the Bones

So with my crew acquired and my general/chef in tow, I thought I'd hit the last yard good ol' M.O.M. boasts. This one was for the critters that was larger than your average troll or above average beastling. This here yard housed the mighty dragon.

Well, I strut out with Mon'Goro to all the "oohs" and "ahhs" of my crew. I figured they were impressed with me scoring the warlord of the waistband. Ha, that actually was a fat joke this time! But it turns out the "oohs" and "ahhs" was 'cause Mon'Goro brought out some of his infamous plopsicles to help beat the heat of the day. I thought I would leave the crew to reacquaint themselves with their new chef, as I should probably scout out the dragon's yard on my own. While I can be quiet as a bilge rat scampering for fishbones, trolls and beastlings lack the more stealthy talents. Now, if I were talking about thickness of brain and stench, then I'd allow them to take point.

The door to the dragon's yard was closed. As I put a deft ear to it to see (actually, to hear) if she was snoozing or whatnot, all of a sudden, I heard the sound of grinding metal. I jumped back, thinking it was a trap, but then I remembered I didn't put no trap here. Half of the door started sliding diagonally down and fell to the ground with a metallic clang. The door, twenty feet tall and three feet thick, was cleaved in half.

Nothing could have cut a door that thick, and so perfectly, without leaving a mark. Only one edge I knows of could have done that: Mon'Goro's demon sword, Gorgutter. Now I remembered what he was yammering about earlier, about him defeating the toughest beings this prison had to offer. My dreams of a dragon joining my crew started dwindling as I walked forward toward the pen. As I climbed over the rest of the door, my heart started pumping, and from the shadows I heard a creaking sound, like bone on bone.

Leaping aside, I rolled behind a nearby pile of rubble. Rubble? By Bor, who's been breaking up my prison? I was pondering this exact thought when in the darkness I saw the dragon. I was wondering how I would get the dragon on my side, when in came Mon'Goro, sucking on the remnants of a plopsicle. He was just standing there like he weren't worried about the hundred-foot dragon watching him from the depths. I shouted a whisper at him.

"Get down, you iggit! You're going to get fricasseed!"

Mon'Goro shook his head sadly.

"Technically, a fricassee is more a stewing of the meat in a broth or gravy. If anything, I would be blackened, or possibly flambéed if the amount of alcohol in your beard sweat was sufficient to ignite us. Regardless, the dragon will not pose a threat."

The crewmembers started milling in and pushing open the rest of the door. When the light shone in, I saw why Mon'Goro was so unperturbed about what the correct cooking method of death would be. The dragon was there all right, a hundred feet tall, longer than a croctopus, and she had a magnificent bone structure. I says that because that was all that was left of her: her bones.

I turned to Mon'Goro and asked him if he knew anything about cooking methods that removed the skin and meat from the bones of dragons.

He turned to me with a heavy sigh.

"The dragon was the last opponent I fought. After our battle, there was nothing left to challenge me. I sought the refuge of solitude. My blade and I retired from the life of destruction."

I remembered stories that say his blade, Gorgutter, is an ancient weapon that has the heart of a demon forged into it.

"You still packing that beauty of a blade with you, Mon'Goro? It would be such a waste to leave it here, all alone," I said all nonchalant-like. I was hoping that blade might stir some of the old feelings in Mon'Goro and inspire the crew with its primordial might.

"Oh, indeed, Gorgutter and I are inseparable, though the path we now tread is very different than before. Look, see?"

From his back, he grabbed a battle-worn sword handle. The blade, Gorgutter, boasted a glaring demonic skull for the hilt, and its lower jaw formed the pommel. I got all goose bumpy when he pulled out the sword, but, just as the goosey bumps arrive, they quickly flew south for the winter.

The normally nine-foot-long onyx blade, responsible for countless gallons of blood and guts strewn across the battlefields, had been broken off about a foot from the hilt. He started doing a mock motion of chopping, but not like he was chopping heads or torsos; more like the motion of someone dicing an onion.

"The key is a uniform dice so that they cook evenly," Mon'Goro says in his most cooking-show-host voice.

All I could do was rub my head. I was batting one for three. The crew looked like they might prove useful. But Mon'Goro was, well, more chef than general, and my dragon was nothing but bones. So that sounds pretty bad, right? Well, think about something I said earlier. Needs a hint? It's about the bones. Get it yet? Ehhhhh! Time's up. Put down your pencils!

Dragon bones are the best substance possible for carving magic runes! Dragons is pure magic at their core, all the way down to their lovely bones.

That's it for Chapter Three. I'm proud of those of you who remembered the bit about the dragon bones and the runes. Those of you who didn't, go reread Chapter One for tonight's homework assignment.

THE ENEMY
An Elfing Reunion

So it didn't take long for me and my crew to round up all the dragon's bones and bag them up. Dragon bones is hollow, so they was lighter than they appeared, and with the amount of hands I had, we made short work of the dumb beast. As me and the boys was leaving the confines of the yard, I heard a familiar sound coming from outside the prison (not the rec yard outside but the front of the prison outside). I couldn't hear the exact words, but the language was very familiar. It sounded like someone gargling a bunch of vowels with a good smattering of *l*'s, *n*'s, and *r*'s thrown in to mix it up. The sweat in my beard started steaming, and I turned back to my crew with a grin as wide as my shoulders.

"Alrighty, you mutts, you ready to earn your keep?"

They all stared at me like they didn't understand the words that was coming out of my mouth. I strode forward, and with a shove, I pushed open the prison doors. I would assume that, to the average convict, this sight would bring out feelings of happiness, or maybe even fear 'cause of being holed up for so long. But I imagined this one was going to bring up some more primal feelings. Feelings like revenge! (Oh, shut your yap; revenge is a feeling. Now listen up before I lose my momentum.)

Outside of the prison, surrounding the *Ol' Girl*, hovered a three-hundred-foot long Unicorn-class Royal Elfin Navy battleship and a company of armored elfs. When I saw the elfs standing on the shore near the *Ol' Girl*, I felt a slight twitching in my eye.

Now, elfs hasn't changed much from the ones I knew in my own time all the way up to these futuristic varietals. They stands an average of about five feet tall and only weighs about sixty-five pounds wet. Every one of them, to a fault, has feathery hair that seems to always be floating in a gentle breeze and is colored anything but a real color. No black, blond, or brown heads to be seen. Only light blue, light green, light pink, and the like. All of them sports long, pointy ears, and some of the more elite of the race have colorful wings like butterflies' sprouting out of their backs, and wee pom-pom antennae like dang bugs.

The crew reacted like I hoped a crew of mine would. Beastlings snarled and hackled up their manes, and trolls grinned, showing mouths full of broken picket-fence-looking teeth, which is always uncomfortable to look at.

"Hold steady, boys, and when I yells 'charge'—" was all I got out before they let out a universal roar of detestation and charged. Now, if the crew had been a more disciplined lot, or if I had explained to them earlier that these was a newer, more technologically advanced species of elfs, well, maybe half of them wouldn't have been incinerated in a dazzling array of pink, blue, and green laser blasts.

"AEIOULLNNRR! LLE ONRAELLN NOLLRAEILLON," came a wall of marble-mouthed mush from the leader of the company.

Now, I understands marble mush to a degree, but I shouted back, "Ain't nobody understands your linguisticals. Can you speaks more normally?" I was just buying me some time so I could gets a plan together.

The H.E.I.C. strutted out (that's "head elf in charge" for you non-sailor types), and he fluffed his hair and sounded out in a quite melodious voice, "I am Admiral Elowwyn Utharilian of the Royal Elfin Navy. We followed up on reports of stolen ePhones and trailed the tracking devices to this, uhh, 'vessel.'"

Now my eyes *really* started twitching when I saw a bunch of Elfin Navy types coming off of my ship with my hard-earned plunder! They were pulling everything out of the *Ol' Girl*'s guts: the ePhones, all the silks and the like, even the decomposing mo-mos. I heard Mon'Goro's breath quicken beside me, and he let out a small sigh at the sight of the crates. At that moment, I came up with an ingenious plan.

"All right, you got me fair and square, ya pink-plumed dandy-lion," says I with as much politeness as I can muster.

"What in the name of—are you a dwarf?" he said all astonished-like. "I thought dwarves were only dirty little fables we told our young ones when they were looking rather unkempt. Well, no matter, you will come with us and stand trial for criminal acts against the Rainbow Crown. Section LRLLWW-1, possession of pirated property, and Section AEIOU-Y, being untidy in public."

I winked at what's left of my crew and then jumped into my most groveling voice.

"Oh, please, your great elf-ness, take me in, commandeer my ship and the ePhones. Only please, please, please leave the old, moldy mo-mos for my crew. They are starving!"

The admiral sneered at me from beneath his crystal swan helmet visor and snorted.

"Are you mad? Have you no respect for your own crew? I would rather they starve to death than be subjected to eating these pitiful excuses for mo-mos. Elfs, on my command, destroy the crates!"

I looked over at Mon'Goro, who is just shaking his head numbly.

"Fire," the elf said with a smirk and a flip of his long, luxurious tresses. His command sealed the mo-mos' fate, as well as his own.

The cannon blasts arced through the air in pink, blue, and yellow scintillating beams. The boxes of mo-mos glowed for a second and then exploded in a dazzling cloud of rainbow fire. I think I got clipped by a plank or something, because I remember falling down hard and struggling to see. I smelled the sickly sweet smell of caramelized fruit sugar and then heard a scream that made my beard stiffen.

"MO-MOOOOOOOOS!" roared the agonized voice. Mongo went plumb crazy, or more appropriate, mo-mo crazy. His already huge body started contorting, and I heard all these snaps and cracks and rips, and all of a sudden, WHOOSH. He burst through his cooking apron, horns jutting out of his shoulders, and his eyes started glowing all demoniacal. Mon'Goro, head chef and warlord of the wastes, entered into the scientific transformation called "going right berserk," and the whole process took two seconds. In the third second, the now-twenty-foot-tall Mon'Goro was upon the elfs.

I was sort of dazed, but from what I remember, Mon'Goro tore into the whole company of elfs single-bladed-ly.

"Ah! Fire at will!" yelled the admiral in a high-pitched squeal.

Elf lasers fired out in unison only to be deflected by Mon'Goro's whirling blade. Gorgutter howled in delight as it chopped and chewed something besides plop for the first time in a decade of centuries. Elfs was cut and quartered on the shore, bursting into clouds of pink, green, and blue sparkles. (Oh, that is probably something y'all didn't know: elfs' blood is like liquid glitter, and when they gets killed, they pop and turn into a tumult of the sparkly stuff.) Anyways, Mon'Goro was a hurricane of purple fury, tearing through the ranks of the elfs. I saw the half of my crew that didn't get eradicated charge into the fight, eager to help their newly revived warlord.

"Halt, you fools. He's plumb berserk!" I yelled at their backs. It was too late, though.

Mon'Goro, drunk on the battle lust, recognized neither friend nor foe, and unfortunately for the crew, he tore through elf, beastling, and troll alike. Anyone bold enough to buy tickets to this theater of carnage was in for the double feature of rend and ruin!

The admiral, seeing his entire company wiped out to an elf, leaped into the air and flew hastily back to his battleship hovering one hundred feet or so above the fracas, commanding that all the guns turn toward the purple doom. In an instant, Mon'Goro hurtled toward the vessel, and I kid you not, he deflected the laser cannons' blasts right back upon the ship! The ship started sagging under the barrage of its own cannons, and at the last moment, he chopped down with his blade. His demon sword emitted a horrific roar, and for a split second I saw the full outline of the unbroken blade glow evilly before it tore through the entire hull of the hovercraft. The ship split in two and landed unceremoniously on the water, exploding upon impact and sending hover-drives and shrapnel everywhere.

Elf ship parts and pretty puffs of glitter littered the shore, and as the smoke cleared, out came Mon'Goro, covered in pink, green, and orange sparkly gore. And believe it or not, the dude was shredded! I don't means like he was cut up in ribbons; no, he didn't have a scratch. I means shredded as in not an ounce of chub was left on his frame. He burned up so much energy in his berserk state—popping about three hundred elfs, destroying a dang floating battleship and all—that, well, he must have melted the fat right off of him. Now he looked like the true warlord of the wastes that he should be.

Only problem was that he was coming right for me. My crew was extinct. Well, except for Gruesome, who must have stayed nearby to valiantly protect his captain during the fight, though at the moment he was hiding behind the gates of the prison and trying to close them.

Like I was saying, my crew was gone, and Mon'Goro, still in the throes of his battle lust, was stalking toward me like he just finished his dinner of slaughter and was looking to order up dessert. I reacted quicker than my brain could process; I had no clue what I was doing. I reached down, and all the while my brain was wondering why I was picking up an ol' charred mo-mo pit. My brain saw me hold it up toward Mon'Goro. In the following instant, my brain caught up and smiled in approval.

Mon'Goro stared at the mo-mo pit, tilting his purple melon to the side in a confused sort of way. Then something snapped, and he looked like he just woke up from some long dream. He gently reached out for the pit and took it in his hands as carefully as one might cradle a newborn pup. (I'd have said "cat," as they is more frail than pooches, but I'm not really a cat kind of dwarf.)

"You will live again, dear friend," he said to the pit, and then turned toward me. "Forgive me for the mess I have caused on the shore. Please allow me to tidy up once I have planted the young mo-mo pod."

"Ah, yeah, no problem, Mongo," I said distractedly. I wasn't really paying attention to what he was saying, as I was focused on my ship,

the *Ol' Girl*. Mon'Goro made it out of the battle unscathed, but that wasn't the case for my *Ol' Girl*.

She laid there with a breach in her hull the size of . . . oh, I'd say, the size of a Unicorn-class battleship hover-engine. Least that was my guess, as that's what was currently violating her port side. Gruesome patted me on the shoulder gently.

"It seems to me, Captain, that we might be staying here after all. Unless the *Ol' Girl* can fly, we won't be sailing out of this prison."

Now this is an example of my brain reacting before I can. Normally I would have belted Gruesome for saying anything remotely derogatory about the *Ol' Girl*, but my brain told me to hold on. It said to me, *You know, Grim, that is a great idea.*

Sure is, I said to my brain indignantly. *Only problem is, how can we makes the* Ol' Girl *fly? She's a ship, not a bird or a dragon.*

My brain just waited for me to catch up, and pretty soon I got there. I turned to my crew (well, Gruesome and Mon'Goro) and gave them some orders.

"Mon'Goro, I need you to pull up the *Ol' Girl* on shore. And Gruesome, you and me need to get dragging some dragon bones."

Ho ho, you guys are in for a treat now. Go grab a pint of suds and a mo-mo or two. We defeated the elfs, destroyed their ship, and sent their admiral fluttering away like a bug. Well, Mon'Goro did most of the work, but that is nothing compared to what happens next. So grab your grub and hurry back!

THE ESCAPE
Fright and Flight

So while Mon'Goro helped the *Ol' Girl* onto shore, me and Gruesome hustled back to the prison gates and grabbed the bags of dragon bones, making multiple trips, as most of my crew had deserted me (to no actual fault of their own). Now came the real work, and I am not known for my herpetological prowess.

If any more elfs was flying around the sky, they would have been in for quite a performance. The first act would find the heroes, Grimbeard and his loveable sidekicks, Mongo and Gruesome, moving a broken but beaut of a ship onto shore. The second act kicks in with our cast running around like fools, placing the bones of an old dragon around the ship. If the elfs listened close, they would have heard such riveting dialogue as, "Can I gets a wing and a thigh combo, please?" and "That doesn't go there. This dragon's a girl." The show had it all. It had comedy and it had drama. And now we will join our cast in the final act, which is already in progress.

"Dragon's head to bow. Dragon's tail to stern. Okay, left legs and wing to port, right ones on starboard. Yep, that should do it," I said as I surveyed our progress.

My *Ol' Girl*, bruised but not beaten, sat as pretty as a pint of promise, dead center in the bones of the dragon. If the elfs was watching from above, it would have looked like a dragon was growing out of the *Ol' Girl*'s hull. Now all that was left was the magic part.

I asked my crew of two to give me some space so I could concentrate but also for their safety. See, I was planning on doing something right crazy in that moment. I fumbled around in my beard and pulled out my old grandpappy's scrimshaw set. I remember when I was a young swabbie watching him carve with this set. I used the very same tools to carve the runes of life for M.O.M.'s stone guardians. Back then, I only used a chip of dragon bone to breathe life into the lifeless. This time, I was using the whole dragon!

I sat there, staring at the skull of this dead lizard, looking for the right spot. She had a big old horn on her nose, and there was a spot just the right size for the rune. Now I don't need to hear any of your yammering about how "most horns and beaks of dinosaurs are actually keratin." Just stow all that nonsense. If it was keratin, then the rune of life wouldn't have brought the dragon back to—Bor's beard, now you are making *me* ruin the story!

So anyways, I was carving away, and I must say that it was flawless. As soon as I stepped away, I felt the magical energies begin to swirl in the air. The bones hummed with power and started moving together. I still had it; the *Ol' Girl* would live again! Bony wings unfurled, and the vertebrae and ribs knit together and wrapped around the hull of my ship. The tailbones started clicking together, and just when the old girl—the dragon, I mean—was about to stand up after a hundred plus years of death, she crumpled to the ground in a heap.

Now I can just hear all you zoologists in unison saying, "See, we told you the horn wasn't bone." Well, go ahead and keeps that up, because you will be eating humble crow pie in a minute.

Gruesome came up to me, shaking his head all sympathetic-like. "I guess we are truly doomed to stay here. Did you do the rune correctly? It has been some time since—"

"Ain't nothing wrong with my runes-manship!" I belted out of a bristling beard.

I walked around the *Ol' Girl*, trying to survey what the problem was. I was nearly ready to rip out my beard when I noticed something odd about the dragon's proportions. Now, a dragon of this size would have a longer tail. Suddenly I got it.

"We are missing part of the dragon, the end of the tail, about this big," I said, holding my hands apart about three feet. "Start looking around."

Gruesome chimes in with his morose, melancholy manner. "Why do you need the full dragon to make this work? Isn't your rune powerful enough to—"

"This ain't war, Gruesome. Magic has rules!" I screamed back. You know, now that I thinks about it, I don't really care for Gruesome.

So we hightailed it. (Ha, get it? High*tailed*?) Well, we searched the bags we carried the bones in and came up empty. We searched the hallways; we searched the dragon pen; we searched everywhere we been and came up with squat. So I wandered over to the yard where I battled with Bjorny earlier, pondering my predicament. I started to feel one of my moods creep over me, and unfortunately, M.O.M. doesn't allow no adult beverages in her presence.

"No ship, no crew, no booty, no dragon, and to top it all off, I smell like plop and dog piss and—" I stopped mid-sentence, remembering my battle with Bjorn earlier in the day. I remembered braining Bjorn with an old doggy bowl, and if memory served me, there was a weird, gnarled bone in that bowl.

"Come on, lads, let's play fetch," I said, and we started tearing apart the yard. I found the bowl easy enough. No bone. We looked everywhere, and just when even my indomitable will was about to break, I heard a laugh wafting across the yard.

"Hahaha! What are you looking for, little dwarf? Somebody take chew toy?"

I looked across the yard to see a black and gold, now-hornless helmet chuckling atop the prison wall.

"Looks like you could not defeat Bjorn Huge, and now Bjorn Huge hold key to your freedom!" said Bjorn Huge as he somehow held up the last damn piece of the dragon's tail.

I looked to Gruesome for any advice, and he just put on that gloomy mug of his.

"It seems we are doomed to—"

I shoved the sack we was going to use to carry the dragon tailbone over his head and cinched it tight. Instead of punching the sack, I turned to Bjorn.

"Alrighty, Bjorn, you win. You wins the fight. Is that what you wants to hear? Now gives me the bone."

(Ha! That came out wrong, but you gets the idea of what I was saying.)

Bjorn Huge was quiet for a moment and then shouted back, "Bjorn Huge not win, but I would count brawl as tie!" He said it respectfully enough for a bodiless head. "Now what do you have to offer Bjorn Huge in return for dragon tail?"

I thought a minute and considered saying something about giving him my old hat collection, but I couldn't risk it.

"How about freedom from the prison?"

Bjorn peered down regally. "How about Bjorn be captain of ship?"

"Ain't nobody going to be captain of the *Ol' Girl* but me!" I shouted back caustically.

Bjorn didn't budge.

"Okay, well, guess I just throw this little bone into ocean. Which spot you think look deepest?"

Bjorn turned his helmet around and was just about to lob the tail bit into the Azurewine Ocean.

"Wait now, bucket brains. How's about a certified rank of Assistant to the Captain?" I said in my most polite voice.

"That not official position!" shouted Bjorn.

"It is on my ship," I said evenly.

"I need time to think about Assistant Captain idea."

"It's actually Assistant *to* the Captain."

"Same thing. Let shake," he said from atop the wall, waiting for me to do something.

I was confused, but I held out my hand and shook the air.

"Okay, we got deal," Bjorn said, and somehow tossed the dragon tailbone to me. I dove and fell into the pen of wolf piss again but caught the bone. As I was rising, Bjorn hopped by, shouting to Gruesome and Mon'Goro. "All right, you slugs, get a move on. We got dragon stuff to do!"

By the time we got back, the sun was setting, and off in the distance I saw something moving swiftly in the sky. Three elfin destroyers were cruising in quickly. They must've gotten concerned when one of their battleships blinked into oblivion off their grid. I grabbed the gnarled, wolf-chewed tip of the tailbone and put it in its place.

"Come on, *Ol' Girl*, I needs you now more than ever, my friend," I said, brushing away a speck of sentiment from my eye.

The tailbone hovered and then snapped into place with the rest of the bones. I saw a charge of magic course from my rune of life and go all

the ways to the end of the newly acquired tail. Me and my crew of three were nearly knocked off our feets when the *Ol' Girl* hurtled up from the shore and flapped her bony wings. The dragon looked at me and roared menacingly, and I looked to my crew.

"Uh-oh. Something tells me this was a bad idea."

Over the dragon's roar, Gruesome started mumbling his mopey diatribe. "It is destiny for us to stay in this prison. I—" He stopped mid-sentence as the *Ol' Girl* chomped down on him.

Ha, that's right. I guess now I remembers what happened to Gruesome. He was a despondent one. I bet when the *Ol' Girl* farted him out, even his fart was miserable.

While the *Ol' Girl* was preoccupied, I bent over and grabbed me a weapon. Normally, I never lays hands on a female, but in the case of the female being a magically animated dead dragon, I makes an exception. Half an oar was stuck in the sand, and I grabbed it and held it up in the air. The *Ol' Girl* stopped in mid-chomp and stared at it, and would you believe it, her dang tail started wagging. I moved the oar from side to side, and her big old skeletal head followed the motion. I pretended like I threw the oar, and sure enough, the *Ol' Girl* ran, thinking I threw it. She turned around, and I'm telling you the truth here, she bloody barked at me! So I wound up and threw the dang oar, and the *Ol' Girl* jumped up, flew over to it, picked it up in her maw, and dropped it back in front of me.

Bjorn bounded over, and for a minute I wondered if he was getting sand all up in his neck hole.

"Bjorn Huge give one of my wolf pups old dragon tail to chew on. Now dragon act like doggy?"

Ha, see? I told you dragons was stupid lizards. A few dribbles of wolf drool must have soaked into the bone when it was being chawed on, and when I reattached it to the whole dragon, the puppy's personality fused with the dragon's.

I look at the *Ol' Girl* and smiled proudly. My dear friend seemed to be back in action, and on top of that, I loves dogs. I jumped aboard my new-old ship and motioned all the rest to board as well. All the rest being Bjorn, who somehow managed to climb up the rope ladder, and Mon'Goro, who was busy planting his mo-mo seed in a chipped and cracked crystal elf helmet.

I scratched behind what would be the *Ol' Girl*'s ear, which caused her to do that cute little leg shake doggies do. Only when she did it, she shook the ship almost to pieces. I needed to remember to batten down more than the hatches when I got some time later. Right now, me and the *Ol' Girl* had some catching up to do, and I don't mean with each other. Those elf destroyers saw the *Ol' Girl* take to the sky, belching forth magical lightning fire, and plumb turned tail. The *Ol' Girl* caught up with them in no time flat. Boy, can she fly!

Well, me being an honorable captain and all, I offered quarter. That is, a quarter of a second to surrender over all contents to their new owner—me!

We tossed the elfs overboard (which was fine, as they can fly, if you remember). I also tossed over a few crates of ePhones, which the *Ol' Girl* proceeded to chew on. She eventually spit them up, as she ain't too fond of elf cuisine. We took what spoils we wanted and split them evenly, even though Bjorny was demanding a greater "Assistant to the Captain" share.

As I see it, everything worked out in the end. The *Ol' Girl* got a hull lift. I got a young fireball of an assistant, Bjorn Huge, and a chef that, when he ain't watching cooking shows or soap operas, is quite the monster. I still can't abide mo-mos; just don't tell Mon'Goro that. We don't need to get him angry.

Well, boys and girls, that's it for this tale. We ended up flying back to M.O.M., and I plotted her on a course about one thousand miles away. It's a lot harder to find her now with my runic compass. It just stays pointing toward the Ol' Girl. Ah, a small price to pay, considering I got a flying ship to harass them elfs with now! Sorry for rambling on, but when I has some good yarn to weave, I can't stop myself till I knits a damn horse blanket—or in my case, a dragon blanket.

The End

GRIMBEARD

AND THE FRIDAY NIGHT FIGHTS

PRE-FIGHT FESTIVITIES
Vacations, Preparations, and Perpetrations

Now, normally I am a hardworking sort of dwarf. Weekends and vacations aren't really my cup of poison. Personal days, float days, and personal float days are more for your lazy ol' forty-hour-a-work-week types. But I must admit there was a time when I was feeling a bit tangled up in the beard, and I decided to get away from the adventurous régime I am accustomed to.

So I took myself a vacation. But with relaxation comes a price. No, I ain't talking about gaining some pounds while sipping caloric drinks on the beach. The price I'm talking about is much more important than having a beach bod or a twelve-pack of abs. (Who cares about abs, anyway? Most of the time my beard covers mine up.) No, the price I paid for my vacation was my reputation.

Vacations make ya soft, and what made me soft wasn't the gambling, the women, or the booze. What made me slack off was the roar of the crowds, the pounding of flesh and bone, and the thrill of the fight! I'm talking about the wonderful art of boxing. I always had a mind about being a fighting promoter and decided it was finally time to give it the ol' dwarvish try.

Unfortunately, the elfs don't appreciate that style of living and have outlawed sports, saying it endorses injury, promotes exercise, and is too violent. So let me tell you now of my little vacation and the price that we all must pay when we stray from our path.

So grab a bag of plop-corn and a cup of overpriced, watered-down suds, and *let's get ready to rumble!*

[Publisher's Note: The use of any phrases, catchy or otherwise, is solely the responsibility of the Author. Any resemblance to reality, intended or unintended, is purely coincidental. The Publisher bears no responsibility for the use of, opinions about, or similarities to any phrase that may or may not be a trademark, a copyright, or registered to such persons who think they can legally protect a catchy way of saying something.]

So, ever since I came back from my thousand-year power snooze, I have made plans of taking back the world from the clutches of those uptight elfs. But sometimes even I gets a hankering for some good old-fashioned fun. Not my normal day of fun, you know,

freebooting elfin ships of their baubles and all that. I mean some nice, relaxing, athletical pursuits. See, sometimes I like to get away from all the violence of my normal day-to-day exploits, pursue some leisurely activities, and let my mind wander and soar. And nothing does that better for me than seeing two brawlers wage war in a canvas ring, slugging

it out till one is down and one can't slug no more. See, just talking about it puts me perfectly at ease.

Unfortunately for my mental tranquility, the elfs have banned all types of real sportsmanlike activities. No more Blood Ball. No more Steal or Steel. Now all we got to whet our sportsman-size appetites is *Staaaart Cooking*, a damned cooking competition show! The most thrilling thing you'll get at that event is finding out what the surprise ingredient is! Who bloody cares? It all comes out looking and smelling the same way at the end of the day, or maybe the next morning.

So now, on my days off, I travel to the local bars and pubs, looking for battlers that gots the goods to make it in the square arena. Renting out local taverns got too expensive for me. Not the rental fees but the damages caused to the joint by no fault of mine. I figured since I organizes the fights and I brings in the fighters, I might as well owns the sports arena the fights is fought in and keep all the coin taken, minus the winning fighter's purse. (Which means the cash they win for fighting; they're not actually purses.)

That is how I came to host the Friday Night Fights (that's what I dubbed our little event) at the grandest arena around, the Chaos-eum! A traveling coliseum of chaos, where brawls is fought off the elfin radar and battlers from all corners of this rock we call *the world* can come to fight and forget their daily toils, and get into some good ol' fashioned fisticuffs.

Since I don't want no interruptions by the local constabulary, I usually find a somewhat secluded area to set up the event. I likes to have them on Fridays, end of the working week for the weak working stiffs. The *Ol' Girl*, my living dead dragon ship, helps set up the arena, raising the huge canvas walls and digging holes for the tent stakes. (Well, after we play a few rounds of "tent pole fetch," that is.) The rest of my crew helps with the raising of the ring.

My Assistant to the Captain, Bjorn Huge, is in charge of papering the town with flyers and looking for any last-minute ringers for the fight. He always gets moody on these nights because he wants to be in the scrap, but I tells him it ain't fair, him being a part of the organizers of the event.

Mon'Goro, my cook and the greatest warrior on this dang rock, preps big huge vats of chumbo, a stew that contains everything too slow to run away, and taps a few barrels of Frog Grog (fermented swamp water and honey). Sewage going in, terror coming out. Still, it's quaffable and hits you like a blacksmith's hammer.

So after a few hours of building and cooking and setting up the merch booths, we have the makings of a splendid night of grub, grog, and mayhem!

THE UNDERCARD
The Boring and the Goring

The evening's bill was shaping up to be a monster, pun intended. The Chaos-eum was stuffed to capacity, and let me tell ya, it ain't because of the roof rabbit chumbo. We'd been doing this boxing tournament over the last few months, and the night's event was bringing a conclusion to our fighting season. One of the two maulers that night was going to make Friday Night Fights history: whoever survives the bout would get crowned the first Friday Night Fights Champ of Champions!

So the crowd was chock-full of the usual seaside, bilgewater riffraff we get at all our events: trolls and beastlings, hobgoblins and other dirty "no need to mentions." Bor's beard! The night had shaped up to be a boxing bonanza. Now, another sort of patron had been popping up at these extravaganzas in great quantities—an unassuming breed that is relatively new to this world. They is called "humans," and believe it or not, they are the most numerous breed walking this ol' rock these days. They just popped up out of nowhere a millennium or so ago, and for the last thousand years, they bred their way to the top of the baby-making food chain. Whenever I goes to these little towns, they is just jammed full of the pink-skinned varmints, and I can't tell ya how much I loves having them ringside.

Humans are a race that is fairly boring to describe. They boast no great strength to speak of, nor are they agil-isticly gifted. They don't have cool horns like beastlings or gnarly tombstone teeth like trolls. They is, on average, a little taller than my like, ain't as smart as your run-of-the-mill elf, but are a bit more intelligent than the standard hobgoblin.

So, that being said, humans do have one incredible talent (two if you count procreating faster than wharf rats). Humans are the undisputed heavyweight champs of consuming. Not stuff like booze or grub or things needed to generally survive. They just love to spend: on anything, everything, and constantly. I mean, they are sheeps guided by elfin trends. Humans is always walking around with little wires sticking into their unimpressive ears, heads slouched over, looking all slack-jawed and glowed up by whatever nonsense they are gawking at on their ePhone screens. They spend coins they ain't got on crap they don't need.

But as a young (well, a somewhat young-ish) entrepreneur, who am I to turn good business away? Hell, I even have a special section that sells high-priced knickknacks, trinkets, and swag specifically designed for my human customers. I noticed if I put a *Limited Edition* or *Half Price* sticker on any kind of nonsense, them humans line up for hours before the fights and buy up everything! Anyone is welcome at my fight nights. Long as you can pay, you can stay!

****

I blasted a few cannons to let the folks know the event was starting. Patrons was plopping themselves down for a night o' majesty! We had two explosive undercard bouts scheduled and, of course, a beaut of a main attraction. Bets were flowing like Frog Grog that night, and the crowds were clamoring for blood. And they got it in buckets.

Unfortunately, the claret didn't start flowing because of any boxing. The first match pitted a local buck, a bull of a beastling by the name of Bront, against an ornery ol' troll called Grufus. Regrettably for the crowd, the fighters was too into the revelries and maybe too into the Frog Grog. Anyway, both of them ended up knifing each other when the ref, a well-bred and uncompromising robot adjudicator by the name o' McSween, was announcing them into the ring.

The crowd cried crimson murder and threw insults, pints, and each other into the ring, and it took Bjorn Huge, my as-mentioned assistant and now impromptu bouncer, laying a dozen of the roughnecks horizontal to settle down the hullabaloo. McSween took offense at the mess made in "his" ring and proceeded to escort Bront and Grufus off the canvas toot sweet. Well, what was I supposed to do? Them dishonest fighters couldn't continue the bout with all their balloon animals hanging out their gut. Plus, they cheated. This is a sanctioned event, fists only.

This ain't war, you know. Boxing has rules.

The second bout was promising. Well, it at least started out that way. The two battlers were a giant rhino-looking beastling by the name o' Rhoelly and a barrel-necked hobgoblin named Morgul. At the start of the first round, they tagged gloves, all sportsmanlike, and hurled themselves into the center ring, clashing with the fury of a hurricane versus a tsunami.

Now a lot of folks think boxing is a game of pure power, slugging each other's brains till they spills out of their ears. Strength is an important aspect; I'll give ya that. But another facet that is not to be overlooked is the whole stamina element. It's great if you can batter down your opponent with some thunder and lightning coming from your fists, but, if after the second round, all your thunder and lightning has turned into farts and flashlights, then you're pretty much done. And much to the dismay of the crowd and your humble storyteller, that is just what happened here.

The two lunks lumbered out at the beginning of the second round, all mouth breathing and spent, barely able to lift their arms up. The crowd was furious and started hurling their insults along with their chairs. The combatants were too winded to do nothing but take the hits and the embarrassment to the grimy canvas. Both fell on top of each other and didn't move no more.

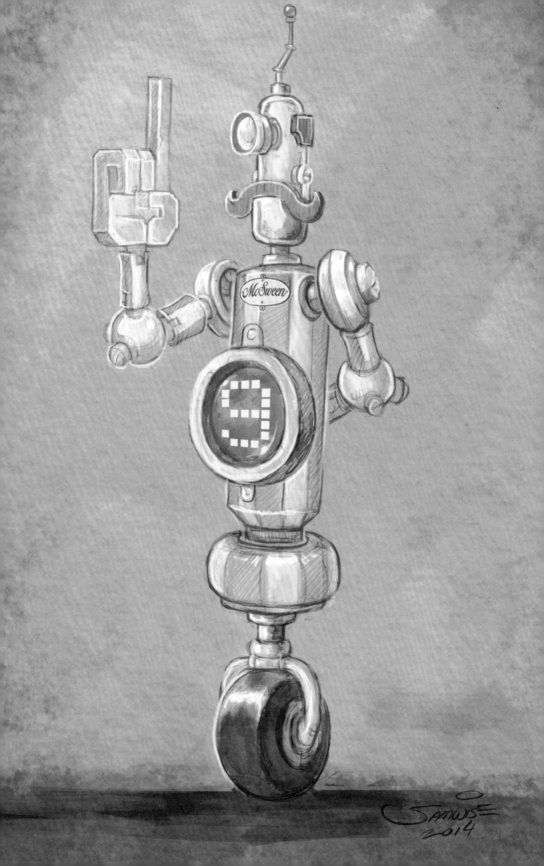

Grimbeard: Tales of the Last Dwarf

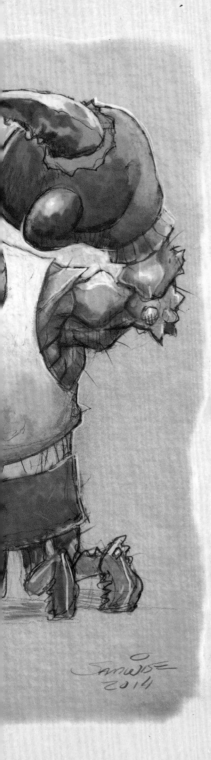

Now, me being the promoter, I had a job to do! This event was turning into a right catastrophe, and since I was captain of this shipwreck, I needed to act swiftly to save my investments and my good name as a fight promoter! I jumped up and steered the winded carcasses off the canvas, dropping them to the straw-covered floor. Now in sales mode, I started my promotions.

"Stifle your pieholes," I said all courteously to my patrons. "This is just what we needed. Now we can stop watering our appetites with this offal and get to the main event."

The crowd hushed up quickly, as Bjorny only had to educate a couple of boozed-up, bleacher-seat champions that thought they had the gravy in them to be the main course. The crowd had been waiting for this all night. The event to come had been heralded as the greatest bout to ever happen at the Friday Night Fights. The two murderers slated for the final match of the night had battled their way into the top spots, and that night one would be crowned the Friday Night Fights Champ of Champions. Everyone oohed and aahed as the slayers loomed in the ring. I hushed the crowd down and announced the fighters.

"On the port side of the ring, standing seven feet, three inches, weighing in at one hundred pounds since he ain't got no bones, we have a fresh face straight from the local sludge pools, a multi-mitted menacing mauler appropriately named Kiiiiid Squid!"

Roars and plop-corn flew freely as the townies cheered their favorite brawler and others booed their nemesis.

"On the starboard side of the grid comes a bruiser that needs no introduction."

I turned around and folded my arms, letting the tension hang a bit as the fans start screaming for the fanfare.

"All right, all right, you want it? Here we go! Clocking in at a whopping three hundred pounds, standing eight feet tall and six feet wide, the dreaded crab-tastic crab man known as Jean-Clawed DeBowler!" The place went cuckoo for ol' crab cakes, and it took a moment for thems to stow it.

I called the combatants to the center ring, and it looked like a dang buffet at a seafood restaurant. On one side I got a multilimbed squid bloke shuffling his slimy way up, and on the other, all clacking and walking sideways style, was a crusty crustacean wearing boxing shorts!

I tell ya, before I had my millenary-year nap, the most I had to deal with was trolls, giants, and a few hundred thousand herds of beastlings. Now, what with all this elfin influence emanating into the world, we got a veritable zoo of critters walking this rock. But like I say, if they pay, they can stay.

The crowd was about ready to tear the tent poles down in their excitement. I looked to the fighters, and they nodded that they was ready. I turned to the crowd and smiled and started shouting at the top of my lungs.

"The Friday Night Fights is proud to announce tonight's main event. *Let's get ready to ru—*"

I was unceremoniously interrupted by a loud clamor directly above where I was standing in the ring. Laser cannons opened up and shot down from the skies. I managed to roll away from the shots, but my poor ring wasn't so lucky.

"I seek the dog known as Grimbeard," boomed a melodious but stern voice.

THE INTERMISSION
Bonded in Blonde

The voice came from a lethal-looking elfin hover-skiff floating overhead, and I couldn't help noticing that it had its laser cannons angled down at me. A hatch opened up on the ship, which looked like a giant mechanized butterfly, and out floated the manliest-looking elf this ol' sailor's eyes have ever seen (which ain't really saying much, actually). Normally, elfs look like a cross between a reed of grass and a dainty dragonfly, but this guy (well, I think it was a guy; hard to tell with elfs) was different. He was a foot taller than your average elf, about six feet, which is a foot and a half taller than me. He wasn't all frail and elfy, neither. His frame boasted lean muscle under his shining metallic armor.

He had a few other features about him that immediately notified me as to who he was and what his intentions were. The first thing I noticed was his hair. Now, normally elfs have a rainbow of foofy color for their hair, light blues, pale greens, and pinks being the chosen hues. Not this guy, though. He sported a mop of gleaming blond hair that was so shiny it was almost clear. And from the center of his forehead was

the second defining feature: he had a long, glittering horn. Yeah, I kid you not, a rigid protuberance that scintillated all sparkly and whatnot.

It was his glorious tresses and that silly horn that told me and everyone in the arena who he was as he flew down on his pretty little elf wings. He landed in the center ring with dramatic flourish. He was looking at me, and nearly forgetting my manners, I addressed my audience with my best announcer's voice.

"Hold on to your seats, boxing fans. Well, those of you that haven't already thrown your seats up here. We are in for a real treat tonight! It gives me great pleasure to announce the arrival of the toughest bounty hunter ever to stride the skies. Trolls and beastlings, humans and hobgoblins, I present to you . . . the Blonde Unicorn!"

The crowd jeered the bounty hunter, but he just stood there, looking all smug and important.

Right about this time, Bjorn jumped up in the ring to stand next to me. He was sizing up Blondie and giving him the stare down (well, the stare up, I guess, since Bjorn is only a head tall, literally).

"Bjorn Huge smash pretty elf. Don't care if she a girl! You want fight? Bjorn give you fight!"

Bjorny lunged at the bounty hunter with a quickness surprising for a bodiless head, and I managed to grab him before he could strike.

"Now, Bjorny, show some manners. We gots ourselves a genuine celebrity here at our little gathering. Why, even the great Blonde Unicorn heard about our history-making event and put on his pretty little boots to come see the Friday Night Fights Champ of Champions title bout!"

I must've got his goat, because he just rolled his big ol' eyes at me and popped out his ePad, showing me a digital display of yours truly.

"Actually, it is the five-million-dollar bounty from the High Elfin Council on your scruffy beard that brings the greatest bounty hunter around to this mangy little pit."

"Five million dollars? It was seven last month!" I said, getting upset.

Now, you see, kids, all these weekends wherein I have been slacking off, playing boxing promoter, have sullied my reputation!

The patrons was getting fidgety and started griping, yelling out loud.

"*Get on with the fisticuffs!*"

"*Kick him in his dandy-lion!*"

"*Wait, that's a guy?*"

I heard them plainly and decided to stop lamenting my popularity and get this show going. After all, my rep was at stake.

"Now, Mr. Blonde—or is it Mr. Unicorn? How about Blondie?

Great! Well, Blondie, I'm going to have to fix up my reputation, that's for sure, and get that bounty back up to a respectable level again, but that will have to wait. I got my title bout starting, and you'll have to leave the premises. That is, unless you buy a ticket."

Blondie must have remembered some joke he heard earlier, as he started laughing like a maniac.

"Pirate Grimbeard, you are under Royal Elfin arrest. You are to come with me peacefully, unless you prefer option one of the 'wanted dead or alive' directive."

I rubbed my head in frustration. I was trying to be all business, and this elf was trying to take my business away with his endless yammerings.

"Bjorn, can you escort Mr. Unicorn off the canvas, please?" I let Bjorn go, and he lunged at the elf like the disembodied head of a tiger.

Now let me tell you a few facts about elfs. Elfs is frail and pale, but what they lacks in strength, they make up for in dexterity. If, say, on a scale of one to twenty, most trolls had a dexterity of about a five, a human would be like a nine, and your average elf would be up at about an eighteen. Well, let's just say the Blondé Unicorn was about a twenty-one.

As Bjorn was flying at him, Blondie grabbed the hurtling armored head in midair and hovered like a wasp over the ropes, pulling them back like a slingshot with Bjorn as the ammo. He let go and launched Bjorn like a rocket out of the arena, over the walls, and into the ocean below. I screamed out the indignities!

"Hey, that's cheating. You can't use the ropes as no weapon of mass propulsion. This ain't no wrassling ring!"

The fighters, who I forgot were standing in the ring the whole time, looked at each other, nodded in unison, and attacked. These two titans were to be my title bout, a fight that would go down in the annals of fighting-ring history. Well, it went down, all right. Down the shitter without a clog, and lasted about five seconds.

Kid Squid launched a slimy salvo of his tentacled fists as the DeBowler skittered in sideways with his gloved claws clacking.

Claxons signaled loudly, and the ring was lit up with laser blasts from above. All the while, the elf looked at his nails disapprovingly.

Of Kid Squid and Jean-Clawed DeBowler, well, all that was left was some stains on the canvas, two piles of ash, and their leftover gloves and trunks—which are completely useless now, unless you know of a squid and a crab that can box. McSween wasn't having none of it, someone firing laz cannons on "his" ring, and he moved swiftly on his little wheel, grabbing Blondie and proceeding to throw him handily out of the ring. Least, that's what I think he wanted to do. Soon as he touched the elf, I saw a flurry of lightning flashes, and the next thing I knew, McSween was counting stars and out for the count.

The Blonde Unicorn spun toward me, whipping out a glowing laser sword. I think I saw genuine surprise in his big ol' elf eyes at being greeted by the party end of my old battle axe. We stood there holding blades to each other's necks for a moment before he spoke up.

"Wouldn't that be considered cheating, my good dwarf?" he said to me all smugly and such. "What with you being a 'boxer' and all."

I shook my head negatorily.

"I'm the promoter of this here gala, not a contestant. Ain't nowhere in the rules it says a promoter can't pack some steel to protect his investments from riffraff."

Now I started hearing a bunch of mewling from the crowd, and I smiled. I couldn't believe they were still planted around the ring! You would have thunk that they would have scattered amidst all the artillery coming down, but no chance. They paid good coin and had been waiting to see blood all evening long, and it appeared they weren't budging till they saw some, even if it was their own!

They started booing and braying like a bunch of pregnant yaks, and I was thinking, *Bor's bloody boxing gloves, my main event is powder on the canvas, and my impeccable reputation is getting hammered again!* In my head, I saw the number on my patrons as well as on my bounty getting lower and lower. I needed to act fast! I put my axe back in my beard and offered my most convincing smile.

"Now, Blondie, you can't just flutter in here, demanding my acquiescences. This here is a boxing ring, and if you means to take a respectable dwarf in, well, sister, you're going to have to fight for your prize. How about we puts away our business gear and lifts up a few fists against each other like real sportsmen would?"

I gave a loud whistle to the sky, and he probably thought that I was just emphasizing my point. I wasn't, and you'll see what the whistle was for in a minute (just hold on).

He chuckled at me all arrogantly. I don't hold it against him, though, as he is an elf. That's just the way they are.

"And what is to stop me from just incinerating you and this whole rat trap from above? The bounty is for dead or alive."

I motioned for him to look up, and his dopey luminescent eyes followed mine.

One minute, his ship was hovering menacingly above, like a metallic bird o' prey, the deadly cannons still smoking from the barrage they just sent down. The next minute, a draconic roar sounded and was followed by a brilliant bolt of electrical fire that arced in from somewhere beyond the tree line. The Blonde Unicorn's ship, which I knows to be called the *Damsel's Virtue*, shuddered, and all its pretty blinking lights blacked out on account of the magical blast shutting down all the delicate computers powering the skiff.

The ship's hover-drives whined to silence, and the crowd started pushing each other and cheering, thinking the vessel was about ready to plummet from the skies and squash me and the Unicorn like a couple of eggs. They got disappointed again, as right before the ship crushed us, a giant silhouette swooped in, grabbed the ship, and started giving the *Damsel's Virtue* a good ol' meet and greet! Dragon bone versus steel and chrome.

"All right, *Girl*, that's enough for now. Let's leave a little bit of his skiff's virtue intact," I said to my own ship, the fightingest undead flying dragon vessel, which I affectionately calls the *Ol' Girl*.

She's a great listener and somewhat delicately put down the Unicorn's ship, though after the tussle, it was missing one of its mechanical butterfly wings, and the bow was chawed on a bit.

The Blonde Unicorn stood silently, and I saw a small tear fall from

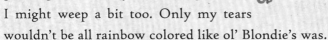

his eye and down his cheek. I ain't
going to grief on the guy for crying. A captain and his ship has a
close bond, and if I saw my ship
get freight trained by a dead dragon,
I might weep a bit too. Only my tears
wouldn't be all rainbow colored like ol' Blondie's was.

He turned around with murder in his headlamps.

"Well, what do ya say? You want to continue on this discussion like civilized folk?" I said, holding up a pair of boxing mitts.

This time, he ain't got the upper hand of dual twenty-inch laser cannons to back up his play.

"What is it you have in mind, dwarf?" he says, silently seething with rage.

"Since you ruint my title bout, I'm suggesting we steps in and fills the void. Last one standing wins?"

I turned to the crowd. "What do ya say, you mutts and scoundrels? You want to see a fight?"

The crowd cheered wildly, and I turned back to my blond rival.

"Ten rounds of boxing, and if I win, you skedaddle back to wher-ever unicorns come from."

He was looking at me with an arrogant smile. "And if I win?" he said.

I chuckled at the mere notion of the idea but answered anyway.

"Well, you can take me in with no protestations from me or my crew. Agreed?" I held out my hand to him.

"Agreed," he said, and returned the handshake. Now, remember when I was telling you elfs wasn't known for their strength? Well, this guy must have been putting in some time at the gym, because when he grabbed my hand and shook, it felt like I had just dropped my hand in an iron bear trap.

We both went to our corners to change into our ring gear and get ready for the main event.

THE MAIN EVENT
An Appalling Mauling

The bell rang, and the crowd was in a fury. They had been waiting all night for a high-class bout, and they could smell that they was about to get it.

We came out to center ring. Now the Blonde Unicorn looked more like a dancer than a brawler. He had doffed his silver armor and came out shirtless and sparkling like elfs do, but "frail" ain't the word I would use to describe this elf. This guy was ripped and shredded to the gills, and he must have had about an eighteen pack of abdominal muscles.

I came out shirtless as well, but since I have been spending more time watching fights than actually fighting, instead of sporting an eighteen pack of abs, I had one big ol' ab that looked more like a pony keg, iron hard and covered in hair. I wore my ol' work boots so my foot calluses wouldn't tear up my ring, and sported a pair of trunks I got from one of my souvenir stands. Man, they were so cheap and flimsy that I might as well have made me a pair of trunks out of toilet paper. (Still, after the fight, I slapped a sticker on it reading *As seen fighting against the Blonde Unicorn*, and I got another sack of coins from the human consumers, Bor bless them.)

Anyway, the bell rang, and I met him center ring. I, of course, hold out my gloves in sportsmanly conduct, and when he went to tap them, he must have missed, because he crashed me with a left hook to the gut. But it didn't faze me, my keg and beard dusting most of the pepper off of it. I smiled back and hurled a right that snapped his head clean off his neck.

At least, it would have if I had connected. As soon as the punch was out there, elfy boy was gone. I looked around and felt a tap on the back of my head. Well, it turns out it was more of what we now call a Unicorn Punch. All of a sudden the lights went out and I was blinded, until I remembered I had accidently wore my hat into the ring. I adjusted my cap and turned around, fuming; nobody touches my hat and lives!

The Blonde Unicorn was casually leaning on the ropes, motioning for me to come over, so I hunched my shoulders and barreled in. The rest of the first round can be summed up as me chasing a blond shadow around the ring, taking lumps in the process, and landing nothing but misses. The bell rang, and I went back to my corner. A ring girl pranced around in a skimpy bikini, holding up a card that announced the coming of round two. Normally that would have been a nice distraction, but unfortunately, the gal holding the card was more suited for my audience's tastes. Well, for a hobgoblin, she wasn't too bad to look at. I gazed over to my opponent, and he just made a cutting gesture by his throat.

The bell for the second round sounded, and as soon as I stepped forward, I was assaulted by what felt like a barrage from the *Damsel's Virtue*'s twenty-inch laser cannons. I knew his ship had been decommissioned and reassigned as the *Ol' Girl*'s chew toy, so I figured it must be something else.

"It's time to end this fallacy of combat. Now all that is left is to take you down, dwarf," hissed the golden one.

I was punched, kicked, choked, and mauled over the course of the following rounds, and no matter what I did, I couldn't get my mitts on that greasy, slick elf. It didn't help that my opponent had wings, which he used liberally throughout the entire bout. Just like the kicks and chokings, flying ain't legal, but I figured he didn't know the rules like a sporting dwarf like me does. Plus, ol' McSween the ref was still recharging his batteries in a neutral corner.

I'd jab and he'd bob. I'd charge and he'd weave. Hell, any time I went to battle him, he just dodged, dipped, ducked, dived, and dodged away from anything and everything I threw at him. I think I was starting to feel his assaults as well, because a couple of times I thought I heard the bell ring, but it turned out that it was just the blows to my head or my cauliflowers ringing. All my vacationing must have softened up my hide, as normally elf punches just feel like snowflakes, but for some reason ol' Blondie's punches felt like snowballs packed with cannonballs.

Now, listen up! This is where another aspect of the art of the ring comes into play. Remember when I was talking earlier? Not only do you need to have strength *and* stamina to be a champeen fighter, but you also need to be able to take a punch (or ninety) like I was doing during this fight. And that, I would have to say, is my strong point. No matter what you throw at me and no matter how many times you batter me down, I'm going to get back up into the scuffle. Also, being a dwarf and all, I has a natural constitution of steel, and steel is hard to break. (Though, after this fight, I think I am showing some dents.)

Well, we continued our little dance, him leading the ballet, whirling in a tsunami of fists and eye gouges, and me taking the pounding of a lifetime. When the bell rang, I saw Blondie go to his corner, so I knew it was the real bell and not the one going off in my head. I figured I needed a different plan, because if I didn't make one, when the final round ended, I would be up to my neck in elfin restraints and on my way to prison. There was no doubting the winner. He was floating all prettily with

his hair casca-pading in the air, and I looked on the wrong side of my normal ruggedly handsome self. One ear felt like a Danish, and the other a cauliflower. My swollen eyes were one of each color, black and blue. Half of my teeth felt loose, and my body, neck, back, arms, and legs bore an assortment of goose eggs, scratches, and purple patches all over like a bruised quilt. I was at the end of my endurances.

Still, I had one more weapon to unleash on the Unicorn: my brains!

I left myself open, luring him in, and after a devastating set of blows (which I blocked with my head, chest, back, and groin), I fell to the canvas, panting like a bulldog in the August sun.

The crowd was going wild! They thought they was seeing history in the making! The Blonde Unicorn was going to take down the infamous Captain Grimbeard, the titular "last dwarf," and sweep him away to the gallows, and on top of that, be crowned as the Friday Night Fights Champ of Champions.

Just my luck, McSween popped up at this time, all sparking and discombobulated. When he saw us two combatants, one standing, one snoozing, he immediately got into work mode and started counting me out in his computerized vocals. His numbers was all jacked up, probably from the bonk he received earlier from the Blonde Unicorn.

"Seventeen, five, shoe—" He stopped his "counting" and told Blondie to go to his corner. He must not have heard or understood, because he just stood there and gloated over me.

"Now, with your defeat I will collect the rest of your pitiful crew: that bucket-headed lout I shot into the ocean, the abominable chef, and that rotting husk you call a ship. I'll bury the former two in prison and the latter one on the pyre!"

He grabbed my captain's hat and unceremoniously tossed it to the canvas. He put his hand up as the victor, playing to the crowd. And you know what? The dang crowd cheered, those no good turncoats!

Now, normally I'd have keelhauled anyone who made disparaging remarks about my crew and my ship. But to top it off, this guy touched my captain's hat, and that I cannot abide by! So while he was glorifying in my ruination, my brain had a crazy idea and my hands deftly followed its directions, and by the time that McSween got to what would have been "nine," I popped up fresh and reinvigorated.

"Shall we finish this dance, my good elf?" I said, and lunged at him.

He rolled his eyes at me all aloofly.

"Will you just give up already? I'll be very angry if you make me break a sweat."

Blondie jumped high above the ring, wings all a-flutter. Only problem is that he got stuck in midair, and no matter how hard he flapped his dainty little moth wings, he couldn't fly no higher.

"What in the—" Ol' Blondie was interrupted by a violent jerking motion that pulled him closer to the canvas and, equally, closer to me. He looked down and finally saw what was holding him back.

"That's . . . that's . . . cheating!"

That was the first time I heard any semblance of fear tinge the voice of the Blonde Unicorn. I'd be scared too if I looked down and saw my long, flowing blond tresses skillfully braided into the scruffy beard of my revengeful opponent, who was yanking me toward him a foot at a time. Blondie heaved, but I hoved back stronger. Let me tell you, kids, elfy wing strength ain't nothing compared to my back-and-arm brawn that I built up from years of rowing. Plus, I weaved his hair in an official dwarfen braid! What's so big about that, you say? Well, allow me to explain! Wait, that will take too long. Let me sum up.

Dwarfen braids are an ancient art form taught to all us kids under the mountain. Not only do they look really cool, but they hold faster than steel links, so no matter how hard ol' Uni flitted and fluttered, he couldn't pull his locks free of the dwarfen braid.

I wrenched his golden tresses by the handful, closer and closer, until he was hovering inches away from me. He realized his precarious situation and let loose with a cannonade of blows. My now ruined mug took it all in stride, as I told ya already about my natural constitution.

The crowd was in a frenzy and was even fighting each other, trying to get closer to the action. The end of the title bout was at hand! The crowd drew to a silence as they saw me raise the elf above my head and draw back my right fist. My anticipation was killing me as well. I ain't landed a single blow on this pretty boy all night, and finally, I would get to deliver at least one good shot! I pulled back my fist, and as I was ready to administer a dosage of payback, I heard what sounded like a metal trashcan bouncing up and down.

Clank, *clang*, and *clank* it came, softly at first, then louder by the second. I shrugged off the annoyance by holding up my glove to the crowd and giving it a kiss, much to their enjoyment.

McSween smiled at me (well, as much as a robot can) and started announcing the winner of the bout even though nobody was down on the mat. That blow he took will cost me some good coin in computer-brain repair, but what the heck, he's my ref!

"Ladies and gentle-mongrels."

I now heard a faint voice along with the trashcan clang, bellowing from the distance.

"No worry, Captain! I am back!"

McSween didn't seem to hear, as he was only concerned with whoever was the last man or elf or dwarf currently standing in the ring.

"The winner of the Friday Night Fights is . . ."

Now the crowd was in a fury. I was about ready to plant the seed of destruction into the beak of my elfin nemesis. Imagine that! The only blow I landed in the whole fight, and it would be be for the knockout! Not to mention that I, Captain Alphonse Grimbeard, would become the first Friday Night Fights Champ of Champions!

Just then I heard that annoying voice that now turned into a roar.

"I save you, Captain!"

I suddenly felt something hit me and the Blonde Unicorn with the force of a cannon! The elf smashed into me, and I tumbled over the ropes and spilled onto the audience. I shook the patrons off of me and stood up, looking for whatever double cross was taking place.

McSween's motherboard short circuited, but like a true pro, he continued on.

"Friday Night Fights fanatics, the title of the winner bout and the first Niday Fright Fight Champion of Champs is . . ."

"You gotta be kidding me," I said with a sideways smile.

The only one left in the ring was a bodiless head encased in a rusty ol' helmet. McSween raised his arm above the bucket head.

"Bjorn Huge!"

Apparently Bjorn had hopped all the way back to the fight and, seeing what he thought was the Blonde Unicorn getting the best of me (which he wasn't), used the same rope trick used on him and launched himself like a catapult. He crashed into Blondie, who just so happened to crash into me, sending us both out of the ring. I remember landing on something sharp and hard but didn't think anything of it at the time, figuring it was a broken chair or a beastling tusk.

McSween held up Bjorn, and the audience applauded their champion with much approval.

"Bjorn Huge win fight? How—I mean, that's right! Bjorn Huge defeat all who stands against him!"

The crowd swarmed the ring and lifted the giant head above them, carrying him like a king!

I looked on and gave a smile. I liked Bjorny, and since I ain't one for adorations, I was glad that he could shine a bit. Plus, I figured I could make some cheap cardboard hats that looked like his helmet and sell them for a good price to the sheeps—uh, humans.

A stirring behind me reminded me of the prior situations, and I turned to see the Blonde Unicorn shaking off the stars he must have been seeing because of the crash.

"Looks like I win, Blondie. You best scoot before Bjorn realizes you called him a bucket head."

He glared at me with them big ol' eyes and held up his hair.

"And what about all this? Untie me!"

So, remember what I told you earlier about them braids? Well, they taught us kids how to tie them, but I must have dozed off the day they told us how to untie them. I tried my best. They are much easier to do than to undo. Besides, some nagging thing kept sticking me in my side and distracting me from my task at hand. Finally, I couldn't takes any more.

"What are you do—" was all the Blonde Unicorn could get out before I whipped out my ol' battle axe from my beard and chopped down.

"*Nooooo!*" he yelled out. I guess he thought I might have been aiming at his head instead of his hair. Come to think of it, I'm not sure which he would have preferred me to cut.

"There, you are free to go. Of course, I still need to figure out how to unbraid all this elfin hair from my beard."

The Blonde Unicorn just sat there, touching his hair—well, what was left of it. It now rested well above his shoulders. It's what you human girls would have called "cute and easy to manage."

I heard this small child crying, and I wheeled around, looking for the kid. Why would anyone bring a kid here anyway? This was a grownup venue! I scanned the crowd, but I didn't see any rug rats. I suddenly realized that the crying babe wasn't no child but the Blonde Unicorn. He was holding a pile of his hair, stroking it sullenly.

Bor's beard, it is just hair; it will grow back. I would have chopped my beard, but it is, after all, the only dwarfish beard left in existence, and I didn't want to dull my favorite axe neither. I straightened up and dusted off my toilet-paper trunks, speaking genuinely.

"Might as well take your ship too, Blondie. I think the *Ol' Girl* is done with it as well. Now, you still owe me the ticket price for your attendance tonight, but to tell you the truth, I think I owe you one for such a great bout. Here, take this."

I reach behind and pull out the annoyance that was sticking me in the back, tossing it to him.

The Blonde Unicorn looked at the horn, then to me, then back to it. His hands went to his forehead and felt around erratically. Rainbow-colored tears streamed down his face.

"You'll pay for this affront! By the honor of my horn and hair, I will be avenged!"

After his dramatic protestations, he floated up to meet his ship in the sky, both of them looking like they tussled, lost, and came out on the losing end of a Friday night. I would see him many more times in the future, and he could never help but bring up our first encounter. He got pretty hung up on it, too. I don't know what his problem was. His pretty locks would eventually grow back, and besides, his glowing horn is surely able to be glued back on with a little bit of spit and spackle. Right?

Well, folks, that is the end of the tale, and also my retirement from the sporting lifestyle. After hearing that my bounty had been reduced, I got to thinking of my future and what is really important. I loved the Friday Night Fights, but not enough to let that tarnish my notorious reputation with the elfs. That is my real lively-hood! Feeling refreshed after my little break from the day to day, I went back to sailing the elfin seas, and in no time my bounty got back up to seven and, eventually, to nine. Now that I'm focusing on being such a bearded terror, I hope to get into the double digits in the next month!

I can't tell you how happy Bjorn was for winning the Friday Night Fights, even if it was on a technicality. Funny thing is that the winner of the bout was supposed to have gotten a golden belt for being a champion. It made me proud to see Bjorn hopping around with it on him like a headband.

The Friday Night Fights is now a thing of the past for me. I turned over the rights to ol' McSween, and he has been making a killing, though now it is more of a "rope jumping, breaking the chair over your head" wrassling event than a study of the fighting science.

I still have some fond memories of my fight promotions, though. I finally managed to unbraid the Blonde Unicorn's hair from my beard, and to tell you honestly, it brought in a pretty good haul. The humans was willing to pay ungodly amounts of steel coin to purchase just a strand of hair of the infamous Blonde Unicorn. Mon'Goro, my cook, swears by it, as nothing cuts blocks of smelly cheddarwurst cheese better than a good ol' Blonde Unicorn hair. Unfortunately, I heard that the Blonde Unicorn's hair never grew back and that he could never glue back on his horn. That is a shame . . . because if I knew that, I would have kept the horn for myself and charged double for the hair strands I sold!

The End

GRIMBEARD

GOES TO A WEDDING

So, there is a particular question that always comes up when I am telling my tales.

"Grimbeard, how did you escape the genocide of the entire dwarfish race by them floppy-eared elfs and end up a thousand years in the future?"

Well, it's a fair question, I reckon. I'm not so well known around the world yet that everybody would know my origins, I guess. It's a simple answer, really. The reason I missed out on my own genocide is that I got invited to a wedding . . .

GETTING HITCHED IS A BITCH

Now, I suppose most of you know the history already, so I won't bore you again with how, after thousands of years of feuding, the elfs and dwarfs made a truce and rounded up all the nasty monsters of the known world and dropped them in a bunch of magical mega-prisons, putting the world in a state of peace. And if you already know that, then I don't need to reiterate how the elfs and dwarfs had a huge celebration afterwards, commemorating the festivious occasion, and that during the festivities, those traitor-ious elfs somehow managed to wipe out all my kith and kinfolk in one fell swoop, leaving only one dwarf left alive: me! Now, the reason I managed to not get dealt with at the festivities ain't that great of a reason. I didn't outsmart the elfs or battle my way free of their armies. The reason I didn't get "got" was I wasn't actually at the party when it happened.

Now, I see your gears whirling around, and I know what you must be thinking.

"Grimbeard, the life of any party, didn't go to the biggest celebration this old world has ever seen?"

That's right. I had a few obligations to oblige first, and after I was finished obliging them, I intended to hit the ol' shindig up and water my beard with a few barrels of good ol' dwarfish ale. But as luck would have it, I never even made it to—

Now hold on, I'm getting to the reason why I was truant; just stow it for a second! The reason I missed out on the whole shebang was, as I said, I had a wedding to attend. Now, I've never been a fan of weddings as such. Having to get all dressed up, wear pants, and everyone is all sniffling and crying. It's like a damn funeral, and by Bor's bloody beard, it is death for some folks!

Well, this wedding was part of a favor I owed to some friendly enemies of mine. See, I am a sporting type of dwarf, and I love me a good evening or two of card games. Now combine that with my love of betting coin and thirst for drinking drink, and you have the basic setup for my reasons for missing out on my own genocide. See, I had run up quite a back tab on account of a few nights of bad hands and *almost* sure things, and, well, I owed the frost giant king a couple hundred thousand or so in gold and gems and the like. This was just about the time the elfs and my folk started being all buddy-buddy with each other and agreeing that the monsters of the world needed to be tossed in prisons.

Ah, there it is. I can hear them cogs grinding away in that dome of yours again, thinking all sorts of dishonest thoughts.

"Grim, you don't need to pay nobody back. Just throw them giants in the clink with the rest of them monstrosities and call it done!"

Now that is some heinous considerations right there. You want me to risk my impeccable reputation as a dwarf, a captain, and a gambling man all over a few hundred thousand in worthless shiny metal and sparkly rock? Ha, you human types have been living amongst them elfs too long, and your brains have been contaminated. I am a dwarf of my word, and if I owes something, I pays it back. Especially now that I am the last one, I really needs to set a sterling example! Now, that being all cleared up, can we get back to the story?

Okay, so we all knows now why I always pays my debts back, but even so, when you owe a mountain of coin to the fifteen-foot-tall, thousand-pound king of all the blue-bearded, temperamental frost giants, well, you should really pay up fast.

I told Ymir (that's the frost giant king's name) the situation with the elfs rounding up all the monsters and giant types, and I made him an offer that would wipe out my debts as well as keep him and his people free from all the incarcerations. I suggested that if he were to forgo my immense debts, I would make him a big ol' floating palace that he and his could live on in luxury and go about undetected in. He agreed, as long as I could afford this deal to his whole clan as well as some of his relations from the fire giant clans.

All right, all right, I'm getting to the wedding part now. So Ymir said that he was marrying off his son to the daughter of a wretch of a fire giant by the name of Prince Zutar. I'd had a few scrapes with this sorcerous dog and his kind in the past, and it never ended pretty. Not all giants are bad, though; frost giants are great. They like to drink and brawl and haggle and trade, kind of like big blue dwarfs. Now, fire giants is more similar in nature with elfs. They are generally a bunch of pompous dandies who think they are better than the rest of the world. And to make matters worse, they are renowned sorcerers as well, and I ain't got no love for dang spell slingers. But if being free of my financial debts meant I had to put up with that devil-bearded Zutar and his kin for a day, I could stomach it, I reckoned.

With a deal in place, me and Ymir shook hands, and when I wasn't supervising the building of the Omega-Max prisons to house all the beastlings and trolls of the world, I was secretly working away on the gigantic floating vessel I dubbed Floatenheim. Now, it was quite a marvel to behold. It was built specifically for giant-sized dimensions, and to give you an idea of what I am talking about, the toilets in this joint looked like kiddie pools. Now, the price to build this boat was quite high but still less than I would have spent just paying ol' Ymir back my gambling debts. It was decked out to the likings of a frost giant king and his royal guests. It had marble and quartz floors and arched ceilings and porticos.

Some of you are probably wondering about how a big ol' boat like this would even be able to float. Well, I had all that covered. As you know, I was and still am the preeminent master of runesmithing. If you don't know a shred about rune-smithing, then I suggest you go grabs a copy of my story "Grimbeard Goes to Prison." (I ain't got time to reiterate all my tales from old for all you newer swabs just joining the adventure.) Well, suffice to say, my humble and impressive skills was able to forge many magic inscriptions into the hull of the barge that would help keep this beast buoyant and unde-tectable by elfin scrying devices.

So when all of the monsters of the realm were locked up in their cozy little Omega-Max prison cells, and the dwarfs and elfs were readying for the big party and genocide the next day, I snuck off to hold court with the last free monsters of the world. We sat in the great hall of Floatenheim, and everyone was dressed up in their finest duds, including yours truly. I sported a nice little striped shirt and a new feathered captain's hat. Now, ol' Ymir is the owner of this fine vessel, but I am its captain, which means I am like the real ruler of this ship. As the last part of my payback, and me being captain and all, I gets the duty to marry up these two kids. I was doing the practice run with Ymir's boy, Jotun, a ten-foot-tall blockhead about as smart as a chunk of glacier ice, and his soon-to-be bride, Pyretta, a red-skinned giantess with flowing hair the color of flame. They stood

together for the first time, and it was clear neither of them was excited by the situation. Jotun kept joking around with his frozen meat-headed grooms-giants, and poor Pyretta just looked at her dainty size-twenty shoes and sobbed. All the while, her maid of honor, who happened to be a frost giantess and cousin of Jotun, glared on in jealousy.

Well, the hours crawled by, and everyone stood up and sat down and said their specific lines and walked at specific times. Bor's beard! Weddings have more rules and regulations than the dang military! From my view, marriage is just like the military. When you enter it, you best get used to getting yelled at, following orders, doing tasks you don't want to do, and asking permission if you want to go out fishin'! That's why I passed on both marriage and the military. I loves females but hates marriage. I loves being a sailor, but I hates the Navy. Go figure.

Well, we went through the practice ceremony, and all the while, the proud fathers gloated. This union of frost and fire giants would put Ymir and Zutar in a dominant position amongst other giant clans. I would think that all the other giant clans being locked up in prisons had more to do with them being the preeminent royal families than two silly rings and a contract did.

After the trial run, the wedding party gathered together in the dining hall for a big celebratory feast. I didn't see the bride or her maid of honor. I guessed they was getting gussied up for the big day tomorrow. Anyway, back in the great hall, big platters of grub were brought out, as well as huge barrels of beer. Ymir and his entourage were impressing everyone with their feats of strength, and Zutar was using his sorcery to animate the plates and mugs to dance around the table. I wasn't paying too much attention. I was just into my eighth or ninth mug of suds, and honestly, I was a bit piqued. Ymir had promised me some festive ales for the special occasion, and all they was serving—at least to me— was some barrels of Meister-Beast, a fizzy yellow lager popular with the once-nomadic beastlings, which, by chance, were now all nice and settled down in prison. It was then that ol' Zutar, who knew the reasons of my being here, saw me minding my own business and started in on me, trying to get me miffed.

"Look how cute our fine dwarf looks, drinking beast urine out of one of our little children's mugs. I guess the tales they tell of dwarfish drinksmanship are highly overrated."

I looked at him with a sideways glance, and then at the mug I was holding. Sparks sparkled, zings zinged, and my cup magically transformed from a plain ol' wooden tankard to a frilly, pink, kitten-festooned teacup. Well, even if it was a giant baby's teacup, it still was the size of a two-gallon chum bucket. I stalked up to the wedding party's table, all gentlemanly like. I saw Ymir glaring at me, shaking his head sternly.

Normally I would have belted Zutar right in his pointy chin and whipped his carcass all across the drinking hall, but I remembered that this was part of the conditions of my being debt free.

I composed myself and left the hall. All the while, Zutar and his retinue laughed it up at my expense. I managed to swipe a refill of beer in my kitty mug, and I swallowed my rage along with the Meister-Beast and went looking for a head. Don't act like I said a bad word, now. I am keeping this clean for all the kids that reads my adventures. A "head" is what you landlubber folks would call a bathroom.

2

THE FIRE DOWN BELOW

As I walked away, my anger was replaced with another, more dire feeling. Fear.

I needed to find that dang "bathroom" fast, or there would be a liquidation situation. That may have been a little kid's cup, but the second one I had just downed, floating on top of the eight or nine I had before, wasn't helping the floodgates. And what in Bor's busting bladder was my problem? I was wandering the halls like some iggit who didn't build the ship! In my dire searches, I heard what sounded like sobbing, like some woman crying her eyes out. My gentlemanly nature took over, and I put my bladder issues aside and walked to the door where the sound was coming from, and knocked quietly.

"Hello in there? Is everything okay?"

The door opened slowly to reveal a tear-streaked Pyretta.

"Hey, how come you ain't at the party? Ain't it being thrown in honor of your marriage tomorrow?"

Now, normally Pyretta is somewhat pretty-ish, but just then she looks at me all fugly like. You know how some people gets really ugly when they cry? Well, we had all ten feet of ugly looking down on me when she started bawling again, tears turning to steam the minute they touched her cheeks.

"My life is ruined. I don't want to get married to that ice-brained oaf, Jotun, but my father won't listen. He would rather sell his daughter off like a milk cow just to get more power!"

She fell onto her huge bed and wept like a giant baby. I never been that great at consoling the females when they is in the tears, but as a proper gentle—uhhh—dwarf, I tried my best.

"Well, just tell him you ain't getting shackled! If my daughter comes up to me, a daughter as, uhhh, pretty-ish as you, and says she is a grown girl and can decide her own decisions, well, even a flame-bearded lout like Zutar might listen. Now, on a side note, do you know where the bathroom is?"

She stopped crying for a moment, but it didn't help with the fugly factor.

"You—you think I am pretty?"

"Pretty-ish. Yeah, sure, and that ain't just the booze talking. Now, about the head—I mean bathroom—you—"

Suddenly she swooped in on me and started landing big ol' fire-giantess kisses, each smooch burning my cheeks like a flame.

"You understand exactly what I am feeling. I feel like I can just, like, talk to you forever."

"You are doing a little more than talking," I said, and started pushing away, which took her aback. "Now, I can't be all smooching the bride of a wedding I am officiating at, no matter how pretty-ish she is. It wouldn't be ethical. And besides, I really need to find a bathroom!"

Now she started with the waterworks again, this time going torrential with the downpour, and the room began feeling like a sauna.

"See? No one wants to be with me. I'm destined for domestic doom with that glacier-headed Jotun!"

Now, I don't know if it was my sentimental side or just that I wanted all those big watery tears to stop hitting her cheeks. I leaned in and held her by her big head.

"All right, all right, just stop crying. It's getting hard to breathe in all this steam. Now, any giant in his right mind would want to be with you. I'm sure any day now you'll find your Prince Ch—"

"Oh, thank you, thank you," she said as she started smooching on me again.

I had managed to free myself from the fiery clutches of the bride-to-be when I saw a big tray filled with goblets of glowing red liquid. I stopped dead in my tracks, and my beard started twitching.

"Is that, by chance, Surturian fire amber?"

The girl maneuverd between me and the punch-bowl-sized goblets.

"I think so. I'm not much of a drinker, so it just sits there, getting cold." She got this devilish look on her face and picked up the tray of red heaven.

"It's a shame you must go. I guess I'll just toss this out the window since nobody is enjoying them."

Now, for those of you who don't know, which is probably 100 percent of you reading this, Surturian fire amber is a specialty brew made only in Surtgart, home of the fire giants. It is renowned for its potency and medicinal effects but is only served on blessed occasions such as weddings, murders, and the like.

My bladder, for some reason, gave me a pass card, and I didn't need to find the head so badly now.

"Well, hold on, now. I seems to remember you wanting to talk about something or another, so how about we sit here, all platonically, and talk over a few of those lovely goblets of fire amber?"

She brought over two foaming mugs and sat down close enough to singe my skin with her flowing hair. I grabbed a mug and clinked glasses with her and poured it down my gullet.

The amber ale hit like a thunderbolt of honey, spices, and toasted malt. This was definitely more quaffable than that swill they was serving upstairs in the banquet hall. As I reached for the second goblet, which, for some reason, she hadn't drunken, I asked her amicably, "So, what do you want to talk about?"

3

JUST THE TIP
(OF THE ICEBERG)

About an hour later, I left Pyretta's room quietly. My even-fuller bladder screamed at me while the ethical part of my brain shook its head disapprovingly. The potency of the evening's festivities hadn't worn off yet, and I didn't know if it were the effects of the fire amber or the fire giantess that was warming me up so much that I was sweating through my new striped shirt. As my search for a bathroom continued, I had a déjà vu type of thing: down the hall, I heard sobs. It weren't coming from Pyretta's room; the only noise coming from that room was the sound of heavy snoring. See, she just needed to cry it out, and now she was sleeping the sleep of a ten-foot-tall baby.

Anyway, the sobs were coming from the opposite end of the hallway, and since I hadn't checked that area for a bathroom yet, I figured I'd just mosey down and take a look.

The sobs weren't sobs of sadness like Pyretta's were. These sobs were of a hostile nature and followed by a crash and a tinkling of glass. I knocked on the room door quietly.

"Is everything all right in there?" I said all delicately. All of a sudden, the door was torn open and a huge blue frost giantess grabbed me by the beard.

"For frost's sake, what do you want?" said the big blue giantess, glaring. She looks at me for a moment and drops me to the ground.

"Ah, you're the wee priest that is conducting this charade of a marriage." She started crying again, tears freezing and falling into her frosted goblet of a glimmering blue liquid. She belched and then downed it in a single quaff.

I finally recognized the angry giantess as the bridesmaid from the practice ceremony today. Unlike Pyretta, she was seething with rage, and I couldn't help but notice how much more attractive anger is than sadness on the feminine face. She was so riled up that her cheeks was turning blue!

"What's the matter, Ms.—"

"Snowflake."

I started to laugh but quickly covered it up when she glared at me.

"Of course. I'm sorry for not knowing that lovely name by heart. So, Snowflake, do you know where a bathroom is?"

She turned to me in a fit.

"Why does she get to marry Jotun?"

I thought a second, trying to remember what's going on.

"You mean Pyretta? Yeah, she is getting married to Jotun tomorrow, though I don't know why. She doesn't like him in the slightest."

Snowflake started sobbing true sobs now, and just like with Pyretta, those tears just fuglied her up right quick.

"She doesn't know what she has. I should be marrying Jotun! He is perfect. He is strong and handsome and—"

"Your cousin," I added nonchalantly.

"Third cousin," she huffed out furiously.

I'd had enough of all this feminine drama for the evening, and as I started to leave, my eyes fell on the tray she got her drink from.

"Well, I'll be . . . You have a whole tray of Frostorian azure wheat ale! Could I perhaps take a mug or three with me while I try to find a bathroom?" I said with all politeness.

She answered in a frigid and definitely non-feminine way.

"No! It's all mine. I am going to drunk and get drink till I can't stand. That will show them! That will show Uncle Ymir that he should have married me to Jotun!"

I was going to comment that getting that toasted will just pinpoint why Ymir should be marrying his son to someone who wasn't a drunk or a relative, but I really wanted to get a taste of that wheat ale.

Since I know you don't know, the Frostorian azure wheat ale is the traditional beverage served at special occasions by the frost giant kings of Frostoria, and since it is a regional beverage, it is never served outside their homelands. I had already partooked of the fire amber that night, and since I was in no way close to finding a bathroom, I might as well cross another of these rare and wonderful ales off my "bucket o' beer list," a list of must-have drinks before I drop. It didn't look like Snowflake was going to part with the beverages, the way she was going through them. There were only a few left and I had to think quickly.

"I don't see why Jotun would choose her over you. I mean, clearly—"

She stopped sobbing long enough to interrupt.

"It's not Jotun's fault. It's my uncle's choice. He would rather sell his son off to the damned flame farmers just to get more power."

I was getting that déjà vu feeling again, so I decided to run hand in hand with it.

"Well, just tell your uncle that you like Jotun and you are going to marry him. I mean, you are way more pretty-ish than Pyretta, and—"

I started coughing uncontrollably and pointing to my throat.

Glowering all icy-like, Snowflake handed me a punch bowl of the azure wheat ale. I tilted the contents to my face and wash away my "cough."

Cold, unfiltered ale brewed from glacier snow and blue tundra wheat. It tasted like a clear winter night amongst the pines and hit me like an avalanche.

"Oh, thank you. I got a tickle in my throat all of a sudden. Now, as I was saying, a pretty-ish girl like you should be the one marrying—"

That danged cough seized me again, and Snowflake handed me another bowl of the blue. This time, though, she snuggled up so close to me that I felt the chill of her body through my beard.

"You . . . you think I am pretty?" she asked as she ran her hand through my now-frosted whiskers.

I tilted back the ale and drained it.

"Pretty-ish?" was all I managed to get out before I got swept up in the glacial storm of limbs and smooches called Hurricane Snowflake.

ALL ALE BREAKS LOOSE!

Well, around midnight I managed to pry my carcass out of the clutches of the frost giantess's embrace. Bor's beard, that dame was built fjord tough! Anyway, bladder near bursting, I crept out unceremoniously, reeking of booze and guilt. I was at the end of the hallway, and I only had one last door to check. This had to be where the head was, and if it wasn't, then by Bor, I was going to anoint it so!

I entered the room and was confronted by the most awe-inspiring sight I seen that night. Giant barrels and kegs lined the walls, while others stood proudly on the floor. Now, normally a room full o' suds would be enough for a dwarf like me to call it a night and waste a few hours in deep, foamy contemplation, but what really took my breath was the two giant vats that sat front and center in the room. One was simply labeled RED, and the other, just as simply, BLUE. In my stupor, I thought I done found the hall of the beer gods! But soon enough, I realized I was just in the storage locker where they keep the food and cocktails. I still had the burning bladder to contend with, so keeping true to my promise, I found an empty barrel. And no sooner did I unbuckle my belt than the door to the storage locker was kicked in, and who do you think was standing there? Yep, Ymir and Prince Zutar, both glaring at me. Each had a similarly colored giantess clutched by the hand.

"What is the meaning of this, you scandalous dwarf? I hear you have been telling my daughter to stand up for herself and tell me she isn't getting married!"

Pyretta looked like she had been crying, but she had a spark in her eye that I hadn't seen before.

"I will not marry that dolt of a giant, Jotun. I don't love him. I love *him*."

The room was struck with a deafening silence.

"You love whom?" demanded Prince Zutar.

I was almost hidden behind the barrel of BLUE when Pyretta points to my general vicinity.

Zutar was aghast.

"You love the dwarf?"

Pyretta pulled back her arm and spoke sweetly but with a touch of red-hot steel in her voice.

"Yes, Father. He knows how to treat a princess, and if I am to marry anyone, I will marry my little captain."

A howl pierced the room, but it didn't come from Zutar. It came from Snowflake.

"That is *sooo* like you, Pyretta. First you had Jotun, and now you don't want him. Now you plan on stealing my dwarf from me?"

"*Your* dwarf?" the other occupants of the room answered, including yours truly.

Snowflake tore her arm away from a furious Ymir.

"I know I told you I wanted to marry Jotun, Uncle. But I was wrong. How can I love a thick-browed glacier git like that? My little dwarf tells me that I am pretty—"

"Pretty-ish!" I yelled as I switched and rolled behind the keg of RED.

Pyretta glared at Snowflake mockingly.

"He would never say that to you! My little captain could never compare a frost walrus like you to me." Pyretta grabbed her nemesis by her frosty tufts.

Snowflake clutched a mass of flowing orange hair and screamed back.

"Bah, the little dwarf loves a real woman like me. Not some pampered fire whelp. I'm the most pretty-ish one of them all!"

The girls tore into each other with a rage that I had seldom seen even on a battlefield! I know there ain't no rules in war, and the girls sought to prove the saying true, what with all the eye-gouging and biting and hair ripping.

"Guards, take the bride and the maid of honor to their quarters, and bring me that dog of a dwarf," commanded Prince Zutar.

Ymir squared off against the smaller fire giant.

"Hold fast. I am king of this vessel," he said in a booming voice. "Guards, bring the dwarf to me, and take the bride and the maid of honor to their quarters."

"That is the same thing I said, you ignorant iceberg!" bellowed Zutar with a swat of his sorcerer's staff.

Ymir answered with a roar and a punch that sent Zutar into the barrel of the RED, cracking the keg so that the ruddy suds poured out onto the marble floor.

"Nooo!" I yelled out, forgetting my precarious situation. I rolled back behind the BLUE barrel just in time to avoid a blast from Zutar's staff.

The keg of BLUE took the attack full force and split down the side, and it gushed its blue blood to the floor. The lid of the massive keg fell down upon me, pinning me fast.

Ymir gave a mighty kick to his opponent's backside, which was answered by a crack on the noggin from Zutar's staff. Now, a frost giant's skull is thicker than glacier ice, and when fiery staff met the frozen skull, the staff split in half. Sorcery is an unstable magic, and when items of vast power, like Zutar's staff, break, the effects can be downright terminal.

Sparks of magic flew and rained down like a fireworks show. One half of the staff landed in the vat of BLUE, and the other plopped right into the keg of RED. Both of the barrels started erupting gallons upon gallons of ale into the air, all swirling about, gamboling around like two flying serpents of red and blue suds. Wild magic flew free, sending both fire and frost giant scurrying out the doorway.

As the magic blasted into wall, door, and roof, Prince Zutar grabbed Ymir and shouted venomously.

"See," he said, pointing at my general locality, "that dwarf is the cause of all the problems! He may have turned our girls against us, but now it is time for payback! Let this magical misfire finish him off. By tomorrow we will forget about him and this entire debacle. The wedding can proceed, and we will rule together and be free of this hairy cur forever."

Ymir rubbed his head and nodded slowly in agreement.

"Agreed, Prince Zutar. It seems I would have been better off just getting my gold back. Still, I have this floating palace, and if your magic works, I won't have to worry about this dwarf causing any more trouble."

With that, they shut the thick doors and left me to face the consequences. The ale started forming up into a vaguely humanoid shape. Bits of broken barrel adorned the figure in mimicry of armored pauldrons and a chestplate. Foam and froth made a strange and probably pleasant-tasting beard on its hideous and liquid-ious face.

Bor's bloody beard, that foul, sorcerous magic turned innocent gallons of the RED and BLUE into a twenty-foot-tall Ale-Emental! See, kids, sorcery is just downright despicable!

The foamy giant looked around the room evilly (well, as evilly as a beer can look). It was half blue, half red, and 100 percent pure alcohol-fueled aggression. It smashed kegs like they was eggshells and roared down at me. All that gushing liquid reminded me about my bladder situation, but I was still stuck under the busted kegs and couldn't seem to free myself. The Ale-Emental reached down and wrenched me loose from the debris, putting a bunch of pressure on my innards, but at that time, I wasn't thinking about my guts busting. I was trying not to get swallowed by the titan of tankards. It was moving me closer and closer to its frothy maw, and no matter how much I kicked and punched, the attacks just passed through as if I was punching a waterfall of beer. The last thing I thought before I got gulped down was sort of funny, considering the situation:

Beer will be the death of me . . .

5

GOOD TILL THE LAST DROP

I was sort of floating around in the innards of the liquid giant thing, waiting for pain and death to take me. It was pretty quiet, though. Nothing was chomping on me, and nothing was digesting me or nothing like that. It was really just like floating in a big bathtub of beer.

What was quickly becoming apparent was my desperate need for oxygen, but no matter how I tried to swim or paddle free, I was trapped in this big liquid prison. My lungs was burning, and in my throes for air, my mouth opened and I accidentally took in a couple mouthfuls of my captor. After a few coughs (where I thought I was going to retch), it turns out that the vile, sorcerous Ale-Emental is downright delicious! It was then that my plan for escape formed.

In the past, I've had the distinct dishonor of being incarcerated (all under false allegations and pretenses, of course), and one of the first ways to escape from a cell, besides picking the lock or clobbering the guard and grabbing his key, is to dig your way out. Well, I figure in this particular predicament, the same theory holds true, except that this time, the digging would be replaced with my favorite pastime: I'd drink my way out!

I opened my mouth and proceeded to guzzle as much of the foul-spirit-ed-but-fabulous-tasting creation as I could. The monster was howling at me, trying to get ahold of me, but every time it did, I simply gulped back what-ever appendage was holding on to me. My opponent was getting smaller and smaller, and my belly was doing the exact opposite. This wasn't helping out the bathroom situation, either, but right then, drinking was sav-ing my life!

Finally, the Ale-Emental was no bigger than a tiny giant kid's kitty cup, and I quaffed the last of it down and let out a belch the likes of which has never been heard on this world since.

The same burp must have alerted the kings to what they thought must have been my imminent demise, and they entered the room laughing. They stood shocked at the sight of me, whether because of my being alive or the size of my belly, which still contained the agitated Ale-Emental.

No sooner were they shouting for the guards to nab me than I started pushing an empty barrel out one of the storage room windows, following it out and hitting the ocean with a graceful splash. The cold water helped wake me up a bit, as the booze in my belly wasn't sitting right. Normally, booze of any nature ain't a problem for my phenomenal constitution, but put a couple hundred or so gallons of sorcerous ale on top of my already bursting bladder, and it takes the situation from dismal to downright dire.

I started paddling with a barrel lid, leaving my beautiful Floatenheim behind me. I could hear Ymir and Prince Zutar cursing at me quite creatively, and I could also see Pyretta and Snowflake blowing kisses and calling me back, before tearing into each other again.

"It's a good thing they have the—"

I felt around in my beard frantically and pulled out a small paperback; it was the dang owner's manual for Floatenheim.

I slapped my head and remembered that I never gave it to Ymir when we finalized our deal. Ah well, it's just the directions on how to pilot such a big craft like Floatenheim. I'm sure they will be fine.

After rowing hard for a couple of hours, I figured I was far enough away from the giants to relieve myself of my current netherregion situation. It was about two hours till dawn, and finally, after a night of searching for the bathroom, I found it just off the starboard side of the barrel. I don't know if I ever have felt so relieved in my life.

Well after sunup, I finally finished emptying my bladder and thought I would get a few minutes' shut-eye before I went to the big party the elfs was throwing with the dwarfs. Even though my bladder was empty, the effects of drinking many mugs of magical living ale finally hit me like a set of RED and BLUE fists.

Blurry-eyed, I could see the gates of slumber dreamily approaching my makeshift boat, so I lay down in the bottom of the barrel and prepared to enter. That was when I noticed that there was about a mouthful or two of the untainted, un-sorcelled BLUE and RED, but it was swirling about in the bottom of the barrel with some seawater. You should never drink seawater, as it will make ya sick. Still . . .

You know when you been out drinking and carousing all night and you get that craving for, like, one last little drink? Well, that urge was

upon me, and so I got my beard down amidst all the muddy boot tracks, seawater, and BLUE and RED foam, and I took that final slurp. Now, the RED and BLUE was just wonderful, but that nasty seawater really did a number on me. I distinctly remember crashing head-on through the gates of slumber, barreling past them to enter the kingdom of oblivion.

Later, I awoke to darkness. At first I thought it was because my new captain's hat was over my eyes, but it turns out the sun was down and the moon was already up!

I never sleeps in late, no matter how much booze I done drunk. I must be getting old. I stretched and flexed for a few minutes, as I was stiff as a ship's mast.

Man, sleeping a few hours in a barrel really did a number on me. And by Bor's gurgling gullet, was I hungry! I felt like I ain't eaten in a hundred years!

It was nighttime and the party would be well under way, but I decided to show up fashionably late. I checked the stars and paddled a few hours, working out the stiffness of my thews. I finally got to the location, a big field called the Plains of Victory. Something was strange, though. Instead of tents and bonfires, I saw this gigantic structure built in some really ugly, non-dwarfen-style craftsmanship. It had all sorts of frilly banners and dancing lights and lots of pointy wing shapes that looked like giant elfy ears. It had a big and what must be magical sign on it, saying (in glowing letters), "Welcome to the Victory-Dome!"

Ah, those elfs must have been extra busy to set up something so gaudy and ineffectual as this monstrosity in the past day!

I beached my barrel and judged my surroundings, scratching my beard.

"I don't remember any of this frilly stuff," I said to nobody, glancing at the decidedly elfin architecture and groundskeeping.

There were crowds gathered about the entrances, and I approached slowly, trying to orient myself to these strange surroundings.

The big sign began blinking and everyone started pouring in, and you want to know the kicker? Every last one of them was an elf (well, excepting yours truly).

Ha, elfs are such lightweights when it comes to revelry. They all needed to come out and get a bit of sea air to clear their pointy heads. All the dwarfs must have been inside drinking still.

As I followed them in, I heard funny comments.

"Oh, is that a dwarf costume?"

"He must be part of the performance."

"That's all 3-D and makeup; nothing is that ugly."

I was listening to all this kind of half-eared, as my attention was focused on a big sign. I read it once silently and now was reading it out loud, and my mind must've not be reading the right words or something.

"Victory-Dome welcomes you all to the millennium celebration! Yes, honorable patrons, it was a thousand years ago today that our world was freed from the vilest beings to walk the realm. On this night, the noble elfin armies destroyed the land's most surly and churlish of enemies, the dreaded, hairy-faced, scruffy-looking—"

"Dwarf!"

I stopped reading and noticed that I was being surrounded by a bunch of goofy-looking elfs. I should reiterate: goofier-than-normal-looking elfs. Gone were their little green capes, the brown-and-tan leather jerkins. They were all wearing the same outfits, which had a vaguely military look about them, and gone were their prancing unicorns and Pegasuses. (Wouldn't that be Pegasi?) Anyway, they all rode what looked like shiny steel horsies that were sporting some sort of

mechanical wings and legs! They brandished glowing wands that they held like they were crossbows.

"What's the big idea of en-circulating me like this? I'm fashionably late as it is. Step aside, ya swabs."

I moved toward the entrance, and wouldn't you know it, the elfs start in on me with the heavy hands. Actually, their hands are quite

dainty and nimble, but you get what I'm getting at. One of them grabbed my shoulder, and I made a point of introducing him to my left boot heel. He started hopping all around, shouting in that funny elfin dialogue that sounds like someone is saying the alphabet (or elf-abet) with a mouth full of marbles. His buddies came in and grabbed me and started hitting me with the butts of their weird wands. After a few dozen introductions from my favorite twins, the fabulous fist brothers, they backed away.

As I turned to finish off who I assumed was the captain of this crew (and get to the drinking), I saw this net shoot out of the fancy wand the captain was holding. Dang thing wrapped me up tighter than an octopus baby in his momma's arms. I tried to un-sequester myself, but this net was magic or something. Every time I attempted to rip free, it shocked me like I was wrassling a lightning bolt! It knocked me down, leaving me in a sizzling cloud of toasted dwarf beard, and as the magic net dissipated, I was left with a nagging question.

"What in Bor's burning beard is going on?"

As I was lying there, it hit me. The funky architecture, the silly clothing. Millennium celebration? One thousand years? I didn't know what had happened, but apparently the previous night and this night were, like, a thousand years off? I know I slept in late on account of drinking a sorcery-made Ale-Emental, but—that was it! It wasn't all the booze that had me in an off way. It was the blasted sorcery! It must have warped my insides and caused me to pass out! When I said it felt like I hadn't eaten in a hundred years, I was wrong.

I hadn't eaten in a thousand years!

The elf captain pranced up all smugly and started talking.

"LLLwyn O'lllollowa El'Alllowlly—"

Ha, I'm sorry; you guys don't speak no Elfin, do you? Well, I'll translate for you.

So the elf captain pranced up all smugly and started talking. Ahem . . .

"I don't know what hole you crawled out of, but there will be quite the finale at the end of our celebration tonight!".

The captain yelled out loud so all the elf folks could hear.

"Take this, this . . . dwarf to the holding pens. After the ceremony, before the five-hundred-thousand-seat-capacity Victory-Dome, this, this 'last' dwarf will be executed."

I heard all this and started thinking, *I can't be the last dwarf. Bor's delinquent debt! I can't be getting executed tonight. I got kinfolk that still owes me money! I needs to find out what happened, and I mean to do it right now!*

Now, this is where it gets good, so pay attention. Anyone need a bathroom break? Well, hold it.

So, sneakily, I reached into my beard and fumbled around for a moment when my captors weren't looking. Finding what I was searching for, I pull out the nastiest-looking—

Bor's beard, look at me rambling on! I think I pushed past the end of the story a few paragraphs ago! Seems I started ranting right into another one of my tales, "Grimbeard the Gladiator"! Or maybe "Grimbeard Does the Victory-Dome." The names are still working titles.

Hey, what's the matter with you? Yeah, I know I stopped at the good part, but that's a totally different story. It's my fault. I was having such fun listening to the tale I was telling that I forgot when I was supposed to stop! Remember, this tale was all about how I missed getting genocided and ended up in a future dominated by them long-eared elfs. Well, now ya know the answer . . .

I had a wedding to go to.

The End

GRIMBEARD

AND THE GODDESS IN THE MUG

GRIMBEARD AND THE GODDESS IN THE MUG

One of the questions I gets asked a lot these days is how come a humble, dignified dwarf such as myself never saw fit to get hitched. Well, one reason is that, at heart, I'm a sailor, and everyone knows that a sailor's first love is the sea. Now, to complicate matters further, I am also the captain of the *Ol' Girl*, the fightingest ship ever to break water, and everyone knows that a captain's first love is his ship. So ya see, between the sea and me and the ship that makes three, well, I am kind of spoken for. But I have to tell ya, there was this one gal . . . boy, she was something else. Skin the color of moonlight on pearl, curved in all the right spots, and she had this curly mane of black hair that shined like it was polished obsidian. And could she drink! So, if ya care to listen, hoist a few with me, and I'll regale ya with the tale of the goddess that got away.

The day started tame enough, I reckon. There was a slight hurricane raging away, and I decided to take the *Ol' Girl*, my ship, out for a morning of foam drinking, which, coincidentally, I had spent many hours doing the night before. The pounding in my head was keeping rhythm with the thunder-cracks when my lookout, the disembodied,

bucket-headed bruiser by the name o' Bjorn Huge, suddenly started yelling out, excitedly pointing to the sky.

"Elf vessels dead above!"

That's just what I needed to clear the fog from my head: a good ol' bout of hot ship-on-ship pugilance! The *Ol' Girl* got all excitable and took wing. Now everyone knows elfs, especially these futuristic varietals, are a spineless lot, but I can't blame the long ears' actions too harshly. You'd all do the same if you saw a boat bound in the bones of an ancient dragon start flying an' chasing ya like a dog does a cat! Now these elfy air skiffs are nice and dandy looking, but they ain't made to take a beatin'. Nowadays, elfs are too dependent on their newfangled technologicalies, and one burst of the *Ol' Girl*'s dragon breath shuts

down their ships' fancy computer hover-systems. Unfortunately, the *Ol' Girl* didn't even get a chance to fart out a spark in their direction, as the second they saw us in pursuit, they jettisoned their cargo into the sea and scurries away.

Well, we picked up the cargo easy enough, except for some of the crates the *Ol' Girl* gnawed, spilling the contents into the drink below. My eyes was gleaming as I tore into that booty (yeah, I loves me some puns). Now I was already in a mood, and when I opened up the crates, my attitude went from unpleasant to downright rancorous. I was looking for stuff any real dwarf needs—weapons, hover-drives, laz cannons; you know, good stuff—but all I ended up with was some sparkly jewelries, ePods loaded with the latest elf techno musicals, and a ton of svelte elfy garments and such. Dang, must've raided an elf prince's wardrobe skiff! Cursing, I threw the garbage to the crew, and the wimmens in particular loved the stuff; least I thinks they was wimmens. It's pretty hard to tell when your crew is composed of trolls, beastlings, and other such vile reprobates.

Now my mood worsened. No squabble, no booty—I'd had enough! I pet the *Ol' Girl* goodbye, hopped into a lifeboat, and cut loose, plunging down into the waves below. Of course, me being a master sailor, I landed the craft with barely a splash and set forth a-rowing. Now don't tell the *Ol' Girl* this, as she might get downcast, but when a sailor needs to collect his thoughts, there ain't no better way to wrangle them up than to grab an oar and stretch those mental thews with some good ol' backbreaking rowing! After a few leagues, I bumped up to the dock of a small whaling town the sign named Planktown.

All the rowing done got me thirsty, and I realized I hadn't watered my beard since last night. After a chat with some local tough guys (who apologized profusely after finding out that trying to rob me ain't such a good idea), they politely pointed me to the nearest joint that specializes in beard hydrotherapy.

Now my melancholies tend to linger if a specific remedy isn't taken every two to four hours, and the last time I remembered my tonics was late the previous night (well, early that morning, to be more precise). I entered a joint called the Filthy Bagpipe, pulled up a stool, and shouted to the bartender, a rat-faced galoot, that I'd take a few pints of his various medicines to see which one would cure my temperament.

Rat Face shouted back at me with not-so-friendly candor: "This ain't no infirma-rarry. All I gots here is suds and grog and poppadums."

"That's what I said, Rat Face: medication!" I said with a snarl. "Give me fifty pints of suds, ten bottles of grog, and one poppadum."

He stared at me in shock, and I slapped my head and remembered my manners. "Please, ya grimy rat face."

Now I wasn't trying to be mean by calling him a rat face, but I wasn't being erroneous neither. This scallywag was a seven-foot-tall, white-furred, verminous rat-man. He watched me go to administering my remedies, eyeballing me with his bright red eyes, all the while washing the same clean mug with a dirty rag.

I took my time to finish up my appetizers while I waited patiently for my poppadum. A storm must've been a-brewing up, 'cause my vision was starting to get all foggy-like, and it couldn't be from the beverages I been gingerly sipping. The good news was I felt a slight twitching in my cheeks, like my smile was struggling to return—hydrotherapy working its wonders! I think the other patrons got tired of waiting for their poppadums too, and over the course of a couple of hours, they started to trickle out.

The only one left besides me and ol' R.F. the bartender was a, uh, female patron? Least I think it was female. (Like I said, it is hard to tell

Grimbeard and the Goddess in the Mug

with trolls.) And this dame was *ugly*, even by troll standards. Last time I saw that many barnacles was when I was scraping the *Ol' Girl's* keel! Now she kept ogling me all luridly and talking about how nice my beard is, and I ain't normally the kind that falls prey to flatteries, so I said to her that *her* beard was just as nice as mine.

I was readying to head on back to the *Ol' Girl*, since she was probably missing me (and besides, my mugs were all empty). I ordered a few more cocktails; I figured I could have one or more for the waves. As I tilted my cup back, I saw something through the bottom of my mug (this was a right fancy joint, being that it had glass-bottom mugs). I spotted a strange bottle tucked away on the shelf like it was trying to hide from me, but I gots the sharpest eyes that've ever sailed these barrooms. Now I am what you call a pioneer of the pints, and I ain't never seen no booze like that before. It was just a normal-looking bottle, but the liquid inside was a weird yellow-orange-green color, and it was glowing all wanly at me.

"What's in the bottle o'er yonder?" I said with wonder.

Rat Face answered all nonchalantly, "Oh, that is just a bottle of troll piss we use for cleaning the brass fixtures on the stools. Keeps 'em from getting green."

Now, I don't normally go for exotic aperitifs, but something about the name called to me.

"*Taroellpiz*? Is that Elfish or something?" I said to him inquizzically.

His red eyes squinted all squinty, like he ain't understanding the words that are coming out of my mouth.

"It's not Elfish. It is troll piss!" he said, all uppity and incredulous.

The troll dame started laughing a deep gravelly guffaw and got up,

sayin' she needed to go to the timber yard, or something about building a log cabin.

I lay down my good coin on the counter and held out my fancy mug with the glass bottom.

"Gimme a pint of the *Taroellpiz*, Rat Face," I said.

He just stared at me all shocked-like, and I was about ready to ask him if he was deaf, but then I slapped my noggin again.

"Gimme a pint of the *Taroellpiz*, *please*," I said, remembering my manners.

He saw my ire was still up from earlier in the day and didn't waste any more time talking sideways with me. He handed me the bottle, swiped my coin, and left hastily through a big ol' rathole in the back of the bar.

I uncorked the bottle and poured the remnants of the *Taroellpiz* into my fancy mug. Bor's beard, what a head it makes! Looking at the glass bottom, I saw a bunch o' floaters drifting around. Unfiltered, just how I likes it. I held the mug up to my beak, and the smell hit me like a sack of heaven!

"Herbal with hints of rye? No . . ! more like asparagus," I said, and then I tilted the mug back and down it.

The buzz was almost immediate. My eyes started watering, and I started getting this warm feeling through my body, and I swears my beard began to sweat. All of a sudden I felt my cheeks turning up at the edges of my mouth. Took a bit longer than normal, but thanks to that fancy-pants *Taroellpiz*, I found my good humor again.

But damn if it almost got ruined, 'cause I heard the galumph of the troll wench squatting next to me. I happened to look over at her through the bottom of my mug, and I got hit by a bolt of lightning (not literally but figuratively). To my surprise, it weren't the troll broad sitting there but the girl I was telling ya about at the beginning of this yarn. Gracing the barstool in all her glory was a bona fide goddess! I lowered my mug, empty except for a few bubbles of froth and some of the floaters my mustache didn't swipe up, and stared at her like a damn fool. She had it all! Long black hair, curves like a battleship, and

when she giggled, she had a rich laugh that hit you like the chorus of
a cannonade.

With a "come and get me" smile, she gathered her hair up and tied
it behind her head, then turned to go. Now I couldn't let this goddess
leave all alone, so like the gentleman I am, I offered to escort her to her
home.

The next few hours are rather fuzzy, though it could be 'cause of
that fog bank that rolled in earlier during my drinking, or maybe it was
the spell this dame put me under with her beauty. I can't recall exactly
what I was spouting off, but I must have been saying the most romantical of canticles ever crooned, 'cause that goddess was all over me! She
laughed at even the worst of my puns and was kissing me up and sideways, and I remember the looks on the people we passed, and they was
looking completely horrified. And you know, I can't blame them! Who
would think an old salt like me could land a beauty like that! My head
was swimming and I was in love, and let me tell ya, there is nothing like
it. The last thing I recall clearly was entering a grand hall, carrying her

past some of her royal guardsmen and through some fancy curtains. As I'm laying her down on a pile of exotic furs, I thought, *This goddess is heavier than she looks!* I reckon it must be her divine flesh that made her denser than a compact, fit dwarfish frame like mine.

Well, me being a well-respectable dwarf and not one to be talking about my prowess, I'll leave out the next few hours, and you can chalk that up to some fine dwarfish seamanship. Get it? After our bout, the goddess rolled over and drifted to sleep, exhausted. I now seem to remember a terrible sawing sound that dang near reminded me of a colossal beast snoring right next to me. But I recalled that storm hanging around from earlier, and I just lay back and listened to the ragged rumbling of thunder rocking me to a good night's shuteye.

I awoke the next day dark and early; well, I reckon it was still the same night. I can't never sleep in a strange bed, even the bed of a goddess. I rolled over to ask if I could see her again, and I got the shock of my life! Lying next to me was that sea hag of a troll from earlier that evening!

She woke up and looked at me with her dreamy yellow eyes and smiled, and let me tell you, a troll smile is like looking at a mouth full of tombstones—and this one was covered in lipstick! She gazed with this wistful quality and started mouthing off something foul.

"You were amazing last night, my little champion. Where ya off—"

I interrupted her, realizing the horror of the situation. She was wearing the same red gown the goddess wore! She was sleeping all cozy next to me! All at once the circumstances of last night seized my brain and hit me like a bag of hammers.

"You kidnapped the goddess!" I shouted at her most unpolitely.

She looked all perplexed and got up with a snarl, the black beard tied up on her head falling chaotically around her. It kind of reminded me of my goddess's flowing black locks, only she didn't have them coming off of her chin. I continued my verbal castigations.

"You saw me leave the bar last night with that gorgeous frail, and you got jealous, as any female naturally would, no matter the species. Ya must've followed us to my girl's abode and kidnapped her. Where is she, you ol' witch?"

Now, trolls are not really ones to trifle with, especially female ones with long black beards and silky nightgowns. She started a-yelling, and just then, three big ol' trolls came barreling into the cave. Funny, I didn't remember sleeping in no cave. That crafty ol' witch must've dwarf-napped me after she secreted away my woman. So like I said, these brutes came in, saying that nobody talks to their grandmother like that and I needs to take it back or else. I was still so perplexed about the whole situation that I was distracted, and they got in a few lucky shots on me. Now, trolls' bones is made of pure stone, but those little swats didn't do nothing to me but help clear my head a bit.

"*Bor's bloody beard*, you're all in on it, ain't ya?" I said out loud. "It makes perfect sense! You all grabbed me last night, as there ain't no way in the world that one old hag of a troll could get me to this hovel on her own. You ganged up and took me to this dive and then dressed up this ol' battleship in my woman's duds and then hid her. Then you all gets your prize: the ol' hag gets me, and you scallywags get the goddess!"

The thought of all those trolly hands a-groping the lustrous curls of my dame got me red with rage. The events are somewhat fuzzy due to my lack of sleep, but let me tell you one thing: Trolls' bones may be stone, but dwarfs are tough as iron, and in my world, rock don't beat scissors. By Bor, I damn near clipped their heads off!

When the red mist cleared from my vision, their hideout was in shambles. (Well, maybe it always looked that way; you never can tell with trolls.) The three ruffians was strewn all about and didn't look to be getting up anytime this week, but that sea hag had gone AWOL. Fine by me, as I never smacks dames, no matter how thick their beards are. I needed to find my woman; she was probably worried sick about me.

I scoured the cave's tunnels and filthy halls, trying to find the woman who had stolen my heart. After a few hours, I decided the caverns was void of the prize I seeked, and I left all dejectedly and stumbled out of the cave. And wouldn't you know it, it turned out that their hideout was under the docks, about twenty paces from the bar I was haunting last night. I staggered up to the joint and dunked my head in a barrel of old rainwater, which helped clear my thoughts. Last night's events were a mash-up of images of swirling black curls and sparkling eyes. Where had she gone? Was she safe? Where was the goddess of my dreams? Those thoughts kept scurrying around in my head like a swarm of rats, which reminded me of something.

I pounded on the door of the establishment, screaming for the bartender. The door opened up a crack, and I saw the ol' vermin, looking at me all a-scared.

"What do you want?" he said all squeaky-like.

I told him I was looking for the most beautiful woman ever to walk these docks. I described her perfectly, but he acted like he didn't understand the words coming out of my mouth.

"I don't recall seeing any dame that looked like that in here last night . . . or ever, for that matter."

Now I felt one of my moods starting again. I had gotten into a little fisticuffs this morning, but it was with only three trolls and was over in a blink of a bloodshot eye. Even that couldn't cheer me up, for it seemed like I had lost my gal forever. My shoulders slumped morosely, and I felt like I needed to go rowing.

"Well, maybe she'll show up tonight? You should swing by, and maybe she will show that implausibly pretty mug of hers again," said the bartender, noticing my pains.

Something the grimy rat face said brightened me up. That was it! The reason she wasn't in the cave was that she escaped! She was probably so terrified that she was hiding out till the coast was clear, and when it got dark, she would most likely head right back there so she could reunite with her favorite sailor!

I smacked the barkeep on the back, and he emitted a rodent-like squeak.

"You know, you're right, bartender! Consider this joint open, 'cause I gots to keep a lookout for my goddess. You know what? Just in case one of my moods tries to settle in, I'm going to need fifty pints of suds, ten bottles of grog, and *two* poppadums, since ya stiffed me the one yesterday. Oh, and better set me up with a few bottles of that *Taroellpiz* again, *please*."

I always remembers my manners!

Well, that's about the end of the story. I sat there the whole day, drinking and dreaming about that lady, but as it turns out, she never showed up and I never ended up seeing that gal again. Ah well, that's how most real stories end, kids. You don't always get the girl. To make matters worse, the bartender said he didn't have any more of the fancy Taroellpiz . . . and now that I think about it, I never did get my poppadums!

The End

GRIMBEARD

AND THE TAVERN OF THE GODS

I have always been a fan of technology. Even before I jumped one thousand years into the future, I was tinkering with gadgets. Back in the day, I would busy myself making repeater crossbows, hydraulic engines, and the like, and nowadays it's all lasers, hover-drives, and other modern-day magics. Magic or science, same shit, different millennium. You know, as fine as these things are, contemporary conveniences should never replace the real problem-solving tools: your wits, your mitts, and your ti—well, I think I'll just leave it at that, what with all these easily offend-ible types these days.

Aside from everyone being miffed over the littlest of comments, everyone is always distracted with something other than what is going on in front of them. Come on, people, ya needs to disconnect sometimes! Ya gots to use technology in moderation! Most of you human types, when ENN (that is, the Elfin News Network) tells you power grids are shutting down because of "random solar flares" (aka strategic blasts from the Ol' Girl's magical breath weapon), you all sit in the dark, staring at the dying light of your ePhones (and slightly larger ePads), praying that your electronic eGod stays powered so you can show one last picture of your food or a silly cat video to other iggits doing the exact same thing.

As much as I am hacking on ya, I admit I ain't so perfect as to resist the allure of a warm, glowing screen. This story will show ya that even a disciplined and focused dwarf like myself can sometimes hit a glitch sailing the digital seas. This here tale is about the double-edged sword of technology and how it almost got me killed—but how it also saved my beard and head from getting separated from my neck!

TECHNOLOGIES AND TECHNICALITIES

Me, my crew, and the *Ol' Girl* was leisurely cruising the Azurewine Ocean, returning from a financially successful day of pirating.

So this is usually where my readers get all excitable and start asking questions about the day's battle.

"Hey, Grim, was it a Unicorn- or a Pegasus-class battleship that you laid to ruin?"

"Did Mon'Goro destroy a whole ship again?"

"Can Bjorn wear a tie?"

Now, normally I would reply:

"Both."

"Just one. He had something in the oven."

And, "Only as a headband."

Then I would have delighted you all with stories of magical dragon's fire, laser blasts, and smoldering elfy hoverships sinking into the salty blue. But this time, I didn't make my haul pirating; I made it *pirating*. We didn't sound a cannon or crack one noggin, much to the dismay of my Assistant to the Captain, Bjorn, and the *Ol' Girl* (they likes the more corporeal form of piracy).

No, when I say "pirating," I mean like technologically pirating, and instead of coins and cargo as the spoils, the loot is thousands of little, insignificant digital files. Now, I know that sounds dull and all, but in those itsy bits of information lies the real plunder! Stuff like music, movies, TV shows, elfin military codes, and the like. Not as flashy as jewels and photon weaponry, but Bor's beard, do them tiny lines of code add up to huge cash! All those music files and elfin soap operas cost a buck or two apiece, and the elfs make a fortune hawking that garbage to anyone brain-dead enough to enjoy that nonsense, which is mostly you human types.

It used to be that the elfs had the music- and movie-downloading market in a stranglehold because they had these delicate and fragile little devices called ePhones. (I have spoken about them before but never in much detail, so listen up now!) So all these music files and movies was loaded up to a digital realm that the elfs named "eTunes." If you wanted to listen or watch anything you bought on eTunes, you could only do that on these ePhones (or the slightly larger ePads). It was a perfect crime, I must admit. Sales went crazy, and the elfs was making a killing. As we well know, humans are voracious consumers and love anything that smells even the least bit elfy. Now combine that with the fact that humans are as clumsy as ten-thumbed trolls and constantly break ePhone screens and/or drop them into the toilet while they are "reading," and I'd say the rate of return customers is pretty substantial!

So I had myself a clever idea to beat the elfs at their own game. See, I don't needs to constantly be destroying elfin ships or palaces to hit them where it hurts. I can do it by striking them in their most delicate spot, and I don't mean their crotch. I strikes them in their wallets, or purses, as I have seen the trendy elfs carry around lately. (Seriously, they market them as a "universal utility satchel," but to real mugs like you and me, that's just a fancy name for a purse. Friggen elfs, man!)

Anyhow, the way I stuck my beard into the elfin breadbasket was by using my wits, and I created something I likes to call the DWoid. I know, weird name, right? It just seemed to stand up well against the ePhone. Now, a DWoid is a stronger and sturdier version of the ePhone that can play all the junk from eTunes and is one hundred percent unbreakable. Go ahead and try. You can crush, mush, or flush a DWoid, and it still will have a crack-free screen and play the music as awful as it ever sounded. Plus, it never runs out of juice, as the manufacturer (aka yours truly) inscribes each DWoid with a rune of power, sort of like the rune of life that powers the *Ol' Girl* and Bjorny. It's a superior and less expensive product all around, and when humans turned over to the DWoids, they just stopped purchasing them inferior, inflated e-prod-ucts. It made the elfs furious enough to start confiscating DWoids on sight! Now I offers half off for returning customers so they gets another one of my little beauties, and the whole cycle starts again. I am sticking a digital dagger in the back of the whole effin elfin marketplace. Hey, just like that famous robber from the storybooks!

"I robs from the elfs and gives to myselfs!"

That's right, kids: Pirating music is perfectly acceptable. Well, as long as you are okay with financially destroying the ones you are pirating from.

[NOTE: *The opinions of Grimbeard do not reflect the views of the writer, the illustrator, the editor, the publisher, the corporation that owns the publisher, the shareholders who own the corporation that owns the publisher, or any other capitalistic, free-market-loving, enterprising person on the planet. We are all here to make money and profit; condoning piracy would be like working for free, and that's just not right.*]

So now that the legalities are over, I—oh, here it comes. I hears some of you out there getting all defensive.

"But Grimbeard, you're hurting the artists who make the music and movies along with the elfs! What about the poor artists?"

Now don't get me wrong. Artists are great, but they ain't the bright-est tools in the—ain't the sharpest bulbs—you know what I mean. Art-ists are all heart and no head. They got all this creativity and passion but no brains behind it on how to market or protect their creations. But unknown to you and to them, they have me, and I have it covered.

To be on eTunes, the artists have to give up 90 percent of their profits and only get one-tenth of the cash off of purchases because of them dastardly eLawyers' contracts. With me, they can put their music on my own personal music app, Grim's Hymns, and they get 90 percent of the take-home while I grabs a measly 10 percent fee for operating costs. Unlike the elfs, I ain't greedy, so I gives the gentle artists the dragon's share of the treasure. Unlike elfs, I ain't got no standing military to upkeep, no cities to run, nor a handsome, thousand-years-young dwarf trying to bring about my ruination. I can stick it to the elfs and help them delicate artistic flowers, and I still make a killing.

SURFING AND SAILING DON'T MIX

As I was saying about twenty pages back, I was setting us on a course to deliver more DWoids to the clamoring customers and thinking about all the financials I was going to be raking in. With the last few crates left to secure, I noticed my entire crew (which is Mon'Goro and Bjorn) was gathered up at the bow, looking at something the *Ol' Girl* was showing them on her DWagon-sized DWoid, which I made for her to watch her shows on while I was at the helm.

"Captain, you come see kitty!" shouted Bjorn Huge in excitement.

Can you believe this? We still had crates of DWoids left to secure down below, and they was sitting up there checking out Cat-Chat, a site dedicated to dang feline enthusiasts! I'm more of a dog person anyhow, so I set my sights to roust them for slacking at their duties and being enamored with such a delicate, persnickety creature.

Bjorn was bouncing up and down like a metal-helmed frog, laughing at whatever the *Ol' Girl*'s screen was showing.

"Belay yourself, Bjorn. You're making helmet dings in the *Ol' Girl*'s deck!" I yelled angrily. "What's the big deal about some kitten?"

The *Ol' Girl* gave a roar at the screen and started scratching and biting at it; good thing it's unbreakable. Mon'Goro threw his monstrous cranium back and laughed through a mouthful of a seaweed and plop smoothie. (Yeah, I know, it's as gross as it sounds.)

"She still doesn't grasp the concept of her new toy, dear Captain. She believes the kitten is trapped in the screen and is trying to free it."

"Or eat kitty, me thinks," said Bjorn, who was trying furiously to bounce up again to see the screen. He was having some difficulty, what with my boot on his head.

"Get back to your posts, you swabs. We needs to stow these last boxes o' DWoi—"

The *Ol' Girl* reared up, and I heard the terrible crumpling sound of metal buckling under us. I was suddenly falling backwards across the *Ol' Girl*'s deck, and during my somersaults I saw the *Ol' Girl* slam skull first into another vessel. She, we, and me was so busy looking at her DWagon DWoid that we somehow missed the fact that we were hurtling toward a 300-foot Centaur-class elfin battleship! (That gets technology a minus one on our scorecard for this story!) I threw my hands out, desperately trying to grasp anything to stop my trajectory, when I slammed up, inverted and inadvertently, against a stack of steel crates that broke my fall and nearly my back.

"Yes!" I shouted triumphantly, until I remembered that everybody was too busy messing with kitty shows to secure the last few boxes. Me, my DWoids, and my curses were swept overboard and crashed into the sea foam below. I heard the *Ol' Girl* a-raging as elfin laz cannons fired off a barrage of reports. I heard Mon'Goro roar something about his smoothie getting spilt, and the sound of Gorgutter, his demon blade, being freed from its scabbard in outrage. A crate smashed me in the head, but a sturdy dwarf fellow like myself can't be dazed by one measly hundred-pound metal crate of DWoids hitting my dome.

Unfortunately, the second and third crates must have contained the DWagon DWoids or a bunch of steel bricks, 'cause them two were the ones that sent me unda-da-sea level for the count.

As my faculties shut down, I heard a clanking sound.

"Bor's barnacles," I bubbled out, "that bucket-headed Bjorn is jumping on the deck again." Then everything went deep black and ocean blue.

A DWARF ADWIFT

I awoke from my crate-induced coma to find myself floating around strange waters all by my lonesome. I looked around for the *Ol' Girl* and the elfin battlecruiser, but neither was anywhere near. Thankfully, I'd managed to hold on to one of them boxes before I was knocked unconscious. I climbed atop the box of DWoids to get out of the briny water, only to realize it weren't salty seawater at all I was floating in; it was just regular old water.

I was thinking about how weird that was when I noticed it was now nighttime, only it weren't like no regular nighttime these peepers ever seen. The sky looked like one of those crappy 3-D videos you sees on them late-night elfy psychics' commercials. Weird lights, geometric shapes, and strange planets was hovering about, and the stars were not the usual stars I have navigated by all these years.

"Ah, my age must be catching up with me. A tap or three to the head like that would never have scrambled my senses in my youth," I muttered to my beard.

I happened to see a golden star hovering close to the horizon, and then I noticed it weren't no star but a flickering light from a fire, and

Grimbeard: Tales of the Last Dwarf

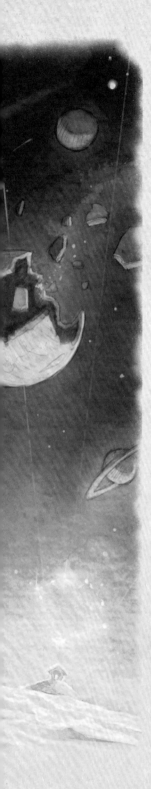

fire means land! I started paddling toward the fire with powerful strokes. Hell, I wished I had the *Ol' Girl* with me. She would have loved all the pretty colors in the sky, plus she would have got us to the fire in a few flaps of her wings.

I was—all right, hold on. I can hears all your inquiries out there. Fine, you . . . Yeah, you right there. I'll take your question.

"Uh, Captain, how come the crates are floating? Shouldn't they have sunk to the bottom of the sea, being metal and all?"

Okay, listen up. Normally the crate would've sunk to the sand a hundred leagues below. But do you remember what the crate is filled with? That's right: DWoids! And as you may recollect, DWoids is indestructible, and because of the excessive amount of "reading" you humans do when you are making with the numeral twos and how much dropping of them ePhones you do into the nasty, I made my product waterproof, and—wait for it—they also float! I told you: you can crush, mush, or flush them, but they won't break and won't sink neither!

My arms was getting a little tired, as it had been a few hours that I was dwarf-paddling on my crate, but I finally made it to the light, which, it turned out, wasn't from a fire but from a shanty. The island that the hut rested on was small and unworthy of any description. I hopped off the crate and landed my boots ashore, and now is when I take back my last sentence about the island being not worthy of depiction. The crunch beneath my feet felt different, not rocky nor sandy nor muddy. I reached down and grabbed a handful of seashore, and I noticed all the pebbles was perfectly round and of some type of smooth, glassy substance. Some of the spheres even glowed with strange colors I ain't never seen before! I pocketed a handful to show my crew and felt around my pockets for my DWoid.

"I'll give the boys and girl a call and have 'em come round to get my boots off this shifty stone and onto some sturdy deck plank."

I checked everywhere—my pockets, my vest, even my beard—but my hands came up DWoid-less. Bor's missing tooth, it must have fallen out during my acrobatics and crate dodging! But no worries: I got me an entire crate of DWoids right here! After a few minutes I was able to break open the box, which was no small task, but luckily the spot that hit my head was structurally weakened, and after a few kicks and punches, the steel crate spilled out my winnings just like an old slot machine. I opened one of the packages, brought out my beautiful little creation, and turned it on. It showed a great connection, a full set of digital "skulls." (All right, fine, that is a plus one for technology, so the score is now even.)

I was bathed in the cooling glow of the screen, and I thumbed over the neat little "phone" rune, clicked it, and then clicked the "buddies" rune.

"Uh-oh," I said, remembering I ain't got no "buddies" numbers on this DWoid. See, this is where technology is a pain. We don't remember no buddies' or nobodies' numbers no more; we just jam them into the phone and forget about it. I shut off the currently useless but flawlessly engineered piece of techno-crap with a smash of my thumb. Minus one to technology for making us not need to remember important digits!

Just then, my stomach called on my internal hotline, and when I picked up, it said that we ain't eated in a long while and suggested we go to the little shed and see if they can rustle up some nutriments for us. My stomach then added another caller, and my brain joined in on the chat, suggesting we have a few aperitifs to help get us prepared for some possibly questionable island bar food. I heard a cheer from inside the little seaside joint, and that sealed the deal.

"What a great idea. Food, grog, and now potential new customers. Let's have us a laugh!" So with the DWoid crate in tow, I excitedly shambled up the shore toward the little grass hut!

NEW DOGS AND OLD TRICKS

I stalked up to the front of the establishment and noticed that the little parking area, which I somehow missed seeing previously, was packed. It seemed like the clientele had an eclectic taste in transportation. Normally, at a juke joint like this, you would see last century's model hovercars as well as a motley variety of electro-beaters and burners that may or may not be up to Royal Elfin Vehicular Emissions code. The vehicles there looked like something dug up from the old fables I remember my ol' grandpappy One Eye telling me when my beard was still in my chin. There wasn't a hovercar in sight, but the lot was bursting with funky winged stallions, magnificent eight-legged warhorses, and golden chariots that somehow had suns and moons tethered to them!

I swear, my head must have took one hell of a beating, but none of them vehicles messed with my faculties as much as the bouncer who protected the entry of the place. At the doorway stood a gigantic fellow, one that made even Bjorn (pre-decapitation) look tiny. This mutt was a freak. It wasn't just that he was as tall as he was wide, nor the fact that he was covered in shaggy fur. It was that this mutt was actually a real

mutt with three dang canine heads on his shoulders, and each one was a different type of pooch. They all had nametags too!

The one that looked like a gnarly ol' bulldog was named Cerci, and the other two, a jackal-headed Doberman and one of them Saint-barnyard dogs, were named Bertrum and Rusty. They was all swathed up in a bright yellow t-shirt that had GOD'S END TAVERN SECURITY written on it in bold letters.

I went up to the doggies but didn't mention to them that their shirt had misspelled *Godsend*. My belly was growling and my beard was in need of a proper irrigation, and the last thing I needed was to get into a spelling bee with a three-headed bow-wow-ncer. Plus, I got product to sell! They looked down on me authoritatively and produced a clipboard.

"What's the name, sir?" said the bully in a charming and polite accent. I guess he was also a she, as the bulldog had a ribbon tied around her head. Remembering my manners, I spoke back cordially.

"Grimbeard, Captain Grimbeard, my fine hound-ess."

The dogs looked at the clipboard, one even producing a pencil and moving up and down the list methodically. Then the heads start shaking. The Dobie spit back a retort in a similar accent but in a less-than-cordial manner.

"We got one name on the list tonight, and it ain't no Grimbird. Away ya go, ya wee mortal. If'n you ain't on the list, you don't get in." After a second, he grins wickedly. "Maybe you'll want to have a stay out 'ere with us."

All the dogs laughed, and Saint Rusty started hacking uncontrollably, finally coughing up a leg bone of some "animal." They growled in unison and licked their jowls.

Now, I am a believer in manners, especially to one's elders, and unless this pooch was . . . Let me see: if most Cercis and Rustys live eight to ten years, and them Bertrum types live nine to eleven—Bor's befuddled brains, I am well over a thousand years old. So if that thing ain't over a hundred and fifty times seven for dog years, then I am their elder and they should show some manners!

Normally I am a dog lover and I never believe in hitting animals, but this mutt was going to get swatted with more than the newspaper! Some dogs is just born with a thorn in their hide. I thought about the *Ol' Girl* and how she would wipe the floor with these pooches. Well, of course she would; after all, she is a gigantic, hundred-foot reanimated dragon, just with a puppy's spirit. That attitude got me thinking, and I came up with an idea based on the *Ol' Girl's* favorite game.

"Now, look here, you mugs. Since I can't go in, do you mind if I watch some videos while I wait for my colleagues to pick me up?" I took out one of the DWoids and started watching. Cerci, Bertrum, and Rusty all take note immediately, as the video I was watching was of a kitten playing with a ball of yarn.

"Oi, what's that you got there?" barked Bertrum rudely.

"Oh, nothing. Just a little device of mine that shows defenseless cats and kittens playing alone and unprotected."

"Are the kittens trapped in there, my good sir? Can they be set free?" said Cerci. She was all princess and posies again. Rusty started licking his chops and slobbering uncontrollably.

I opened up my handy crate and pulled out another DWoid. On this one, I loaded up another flick for the pooches, this one showing a kitty playing with a piece of tape stuck to his tail. I started moving my hands around, and the three heads began following the DWoids just like the *Ol' Girl* does with a stick. Can ya see where I'm going here? Give it a moment.

I fake threw one DWoid and then fake threw the other in the opposite direction. Cerci followed the first and smashed her head into Bertrum and Rusty, who were both following the second. Now I pulled out a third DWoid and loaded up a video that had about twenty kittens rolling around in a blanket. This got the mutts a-howling, as it must have looked like a dang cat-filled burrito!

With their minds all whipped up in a frenzy, I threw the DWoids in three different directions. Cerci charged left, Bertrum bobbed right, and Rusty started running around in circles. As you can imagine, all that turned into a big stumbling match with the dogs howling and biting at each other, what with each head wanting to go his and her own way. As they rolled down the coast, I hoisted up my crate, smiled, and went into the bar.

THE GOD'S END

I walked in, much to the unnotice-ment of the patrons. I was glad, too, because they would have seen me standing there in a state that most nobody ever sees me in . . . a state of shock. I must *really* have taken a smash to the head earlier, as my eyes were lying to my brain and to the rest of me as to what they was seeing. From the outside, this looked like nothing more than a decrepit old hut, but the inside sprawled out massively into what looked like a multitiered hall the size of my old fighting arena, the Chaos-eum. (Check out "Grimbeard and the Friday Night Fights" if'n you don't understand what I am talking about.)

Sitting around the humongous room was a variety of patrons in various states of inebriation and repose. Now, there was a ton of downright oddballs hanging out at this bar tonight. Over to my right sat a red-bearded barbarian type who was spinning around a glowing hammer and ruefully swilling drink out of an ale horn. Over at a nearby table sat the dang ugliest and fattest troll you've ever seen; his shadow alone needed five or six chairs to sit on, and he was devouring joints of pig and whole wheels of cheese in two or three bites. There were multi-limbed guys and gals, furry critters, and big walking plant-type brutes sprouting weird flowers that I had never seen before.

Everyone looked like they were wearing costumes or something, but out of all of them, there was a particular group that got my attention. Not because they looked like they was dressed up for a circus, but because I always recognizes my enemies. In a shadowy corner near some crates and goods sat a group of elfs. But these boys were different. They weren't the newfangled dandelions you see nowadays. They were the old-world types my grandpappy told me he knew from when he was just a short beard. None of the group had pink-and-teal hair or fancy, frilly clothing. These elfs looked primal, wild, and fierce, wearing feathers in their manes and striped war paint on their leonine faces. They was the only ones that noticed me when I walked in, and I quickly sat down at an empty barstool, trying to get them predatory amber eyes off of my hide.

I set my steel crate down and looked around for a remedy for my thirsty and my hungry. There was live music raging, and the band, Donnie Rio and the Profits of Doom, was tearing into a song that packed the dance floor. While I was watching the mosh pit, I heard a loud belch, and a hog-and-cheese-greased hand slammed down on my crate. (Good thing them DWoids is unbreakable!) I turned around and gazed face-to-belly at the behemoth of a troll I was describing to ya earlier.

"You in *my* seat, beardling. Me don't like your kind stinking up my seats," gurgled the massive troll through a series of belches.

Well, me being the gentle-mannered dwarf that I am, I got up and scooched over to the next seat, not trying to make any trouble.

"You in *my* seat!" repeated my new friend as he smashed the crate again.

"Well, what about this seat?" I said innocently as I pointed over to another chair.

"No, that my seat too!" bellowed the big troll through a mouthful of pig knuckle.

Now I was getting right tired of these shenanigans, and when I'm tired, I can get a bit ornery. I walked to another chair.

"What about this one?" I said, stoking the fires, but as you well know, trolls are as smart as the stone they is hewn from, and he don't get it.

Grimbeard and the Tavern of the Gods

This chair-ade went on for another ten minutes, till some of the other patrons was yelling for him to squash me or let me sit. I think he was about to do the first suggestion, seeing as he picked me up bodily and roared in my face. I was just about to give the troll his chair, right across the nose, when we was interrupted by a stern command.

"Let him be, Glubb'gar."

I looked down from my vantage point and saw it was one of the amber-eyed elfs from earlier.

"Glubb'gar not listen to puny elf. Glubb'gar fight both dwarf and elfling!"

From behind the mountain of flesh, three of the elf's companions materialized out of the shadows, leaf-shaped blades nicking at his beefy back. His stomach made a terrible groan, and a ripping sound came from the rear of the troll, clearing the elfs.

Glubb'gar dropped me like a bag of hammers and held his stomach. Sweat was rolling down his brow, and his face was contorting like he was uncomfortable in the nether regions.

"Before fight, Glubb'gar need to do troll business! Let's wait till my mates get off work. Then we fight more 'bout this."

The elfs waited while Glubb'gar maneuvered around his "chair-itory" and went through a door marked GODDESSES. There was a scream, and Glubb'gar ran out and slammed through the door marked GODS. I laughed at the whole thing, as trolls ain't known for their brains. I bet he barely knows the difference between the standard men's and women's bathroom doors, let alone these strangely named ones.

The elfs whisked me back to their table and offered me a seat. I was quite puzzled at the events that were taking place. The main elf sized me up and introduced himself.

"I am Lionheart, leader of the elfin gods who reside here. I know our kinds rarely join forces, but here at God's End, things are different." He looked at me and laughed gloomily. "It seems all races are afflicted by this techno-plague. Elf, troll, and now even dwarf. The world is doomed. So what is—or should I say, what was—your particular sphere of influence, dwarf? Stone? Battle? I'd say, based on that narrow escape with Glubb'gar, you are the god of luck."

I was looking at him like I don't understand the words that are coming out of his mouth. Gods? Spheres of flatulence or whatever he said?

Lionheart shook his head and smiled.

"I'm sorry. You must be rather distraught and tired. How about we order you a liquid respite and a warm meal to help you adjust to your new home?"

I was about to ask how much he had been drinking, what with all the crazy mumbo jumbo he was spouting, but he stood up and beckoned to a server.

"Hey, Grandma? A round of drinks and food for the table, and probably a few dozen mugs of ale for our newest tenant."

What the hell was going on here? I was sharing a table with the most deadly group of elfs I have ever seen, and they were buying me cocktails and chow? And to top it off, they lived with their grandma?

Our drinks arrived swiftly and were brought out by a little ol' gal, "Grandma," I suppose. She had a poof of fluffy white hair on her head and small dark eyes that sparkled like black pearls. She carried a huge tray with tankards, mugs, and bottles that looked like they weighed more than she did.

"Grandma runs the kitchen here at God's End. She can cook you anything you desire, as long as you behave like a gentleman."

"Here you go, boys. I got beans and stuffed artichokes coming up next. Now keep those elbows off the table." With that last part, she beamed those sparkly black orbs at us, and me and the elfs all removed our elbows from the table and set them on our laps.

Well, I guess I can always use some work with my manners.

6

EVERY GOD HAS HIS DAY

I grabbed a mug and busied myself with watering my chin blanket. After a few slugs, I noted that the beer was unlike anything I ever tasted before. Every mouthful was a different flavor: nutty, foamy, hoppy, and fruity. I glugged down a few more, and they all tasted wonderfully new and magic like the first.

Grandma came by with a huge tray of what looked like spiky flowers stuffed with breadcrumbs and a bubbling pot of red beans. The aromas hit me like a sledgehammer, as did Grandma, seeing as I had my elbows on the table again. I fell to the comestibles and ended up devouring most of the pot of beans by myself, plus about a dozen of the stuffed artichokes. When she came back to fill our mugs, I had to give the lady a proper compliment.

"Now, Grandma, I have to say that this is *the* best grub I have ever chawed upon in my life! My chef, Mon'Goro, would kill to get these recipes if you're willing to share them."

"Well, thank you, baby boy. I just start with a few vegetables"—I later found out these strange vegetables were called onions, garlic, and red peppers, and were indigenous to the island—"and then I let them simmer . . ."

Her smile faded as her black spheres bored into my brain, and I quickly removed my elbows from the table. The smile returned, and she asked if some of Lionheart's crew could help her carry a few crates of the aforementioned veggies back to the kitchen area.

The band was playing and the drinks started flowing, and all the while, oddities kept drifting in. A half-man, half-horse strutted through the entrance with all kinds of little female tree people riding on his back. He was trailed by a slobbering mass of tentacles that floated around like a jellyfish and oozed all over the floor. They both were followed by a winged dude with green skin and an elephant's head. I was completely out of my mind. I knew it wasn't the booze affecting me neither, as all these crazy people been coming and going since before I started my cocktails. I looked to my elfin companion for assistance.

"Is there a costume party going on tonight or something? Who are all these crazy-looking individuals, and what are they doing in a joint like this, Mr. Lionheart?" I paused after I said his name, as it sounded vaguely familiar.

He looked at me, all perplexed or somewhat schnockered. "Well, it's always happy hour at the God's End Tavern, so at the end of the day, all the forgotten gather together to drown their sorrows and mourn the loss of our divine divinity."

"No, I mean what are all these crazy folks coming to the Godsend Ta—"

"God's End," he stated somewhat woozily.

"That's what I said: Godsen—"

"No, not Godsend . . . It is the . . . God's . . . End!" Lionheart stood up and glared down at me. "Do you really not know why you are here, dwarf? Everyone you see here tonight is, or shall I say, was, once a great and powerful deity . . . This is the place where all gods one day end up when their faithful followers stop believing in them. One millennium, you are worshipped and loved by millions; the next millennium, you are a character in a book of fables." He drained his mug and set it on the table, and then a coaster, as Grandma was always watching.

The customers all looked up, some nodding, some snarling into their mugs. Some was even shedding tears.

I was flabbergasted. These people must have started drinking well before I shambled in here. My mouth had all kinds of questions that it completely forgot to check with my brain before asking.

"If you are all gods, why are you in here? I mean, if indeed you are all divine beings, you ain't making good on your legends. Ain't gods supposed to be all heroic and powerful, not ... not that?" I said as I points to Glubb'gar, who was crying in the corner, cradling all his chairs.

The crowd started fuming at me, and I'm not ashamed to admit this ain't the first time I turned the patrons of a bar mutinous against me.

"I figure I am either dreaming, brain damaged, or—wait, this has to be a setup, right? That's it! I bet Bjorn and Mongo put these guys up to it to try and make me look the fool! Well, nobody puts one over on Grimbeard!"

I looked around the room and under the tables for any signs of hidden cameras. I didn't find any, but I was half-crocked and thrice-knocked,

so I don't blame myself for my ocular inefficiencies. Lionheart, and the bar as a whole, was getting all uppity at my tirade, but I am not one to fragment a sentence.

"So tell me, Lionheart, if you guys were so revered and loved, how is it you lost all your followers?" Ha, I knew that would stick it to him. I could see him about to boil over, but he calmed himself and proceeded to explain to me like a parent would an ignorant child.

"Since you are apparently in shock and are having difficulty with the transition to your new place of residence, I will allow this moment of impudence . . . but only once." The place got all quiet, and the crowd scooched in to hear. Lionheart's voice was the only sound in the tavern.

"When the world was new and the faithful had questions, it was *we* who provided them with the answers. Over the millennia, the population increased and evolved. New gods were born as new civilizations grew and prospered. From caves and swamps, they moved to wooden huts, and eventually to stone cities. With their industrialization came schools and colleges that taught them new ideas that contradicted the lessons we once taught. Our faithful became more educated and, over the ages, more arrogant. They started thinking they knew all the answers and did not need to rely on 'fairy tales' anymore. Without our followers, we grew weak. Our divine powers faltered and failed. We could no longer walk the halls of the gods, nor could we reside among mortals. That is why we have ended up here. We have become obsolete."

The barroom was silent, but I could see the sorrow of the gods— hey, that's a good name for a band!—hanging in the air like pipe smoke. Lionheart composed himself and continued.

"Why, after so many years, did our faithful abandon us? Because they stopped kneeling before the old gods and instead slouched and stooped to new ones. Hands were no longer clasped in prayer but clutched little rectangular boxes. Their eyes no longer remained closed during worship but stared, open and unblinking. The light of the gods was replaced by the sterile glow of their modern deity. They adored it. Their lives were ruled by it! All the answers, to any question imaginable, were provided to them by this new age messiah called—"

Lionheart was a bit pickled on island-berry wine and stumbled into my crate of DWoids, which spilled out and landed on the floor in front of him. The crowd gasped, and Lionheart looked at me in disbelief as he slowly picked up a DWoid. At that moment, I saw his teeth lengthen, and his hand that clutched the DWoid grew talons where once finger-nails used to be. His overall demeanor shifted to something more feline, and his war paint now looked more like dang tiger stripes!

"You ask why did we, the greatest and most powerful beings ever to roam the astral seas, become obsolete. Because of a cheap plastic idol the elfs created called the ePhone!"

His eyes turned into amber fire, and he roared. He clutched the DWoid in both hands and broke it in two!

That's right. You heard me correctly: Lionheart broke the previously unbreakable. Minus one for technology.

DIVINE INTERVENTION

In a second he was upon me, and never in my life have I been so—is *startled* the right word?

"Now wait a minute! This ain't no ePho—" For some reason my voice cracked, most likely because of the spicy peppers . . . not because I was just a teensy bit startled.

"Silence, beardling!" snarled Lionheart, and suddenly I remember where I heard that name before!

Lionheart was the ancient elf god of the hunt. My ol' grandpappy told me stories about him when I was really young, about how he was the offspring of a sun lion and an elf princess or some other nonse— well . . . maybe not so much nonsense?

I saw the broken DWoid, and suddenly my startled-ness was replaced with a different feeling: anger! I had just heard Lionheart, god or not, associate my DWoid with a piece of subpar elfin technology! Now that just gets my beard in a bristle and is an insult I cannot stand for . . . Well, he was holding me aloft, so I couldn't stand anyway, even if I wanted to.

Lionheart held me up to the crowd like a hunter showing off his catch. The crowd seemed just as prickly about the whole incident, and they were calling for my ruination. It was in those precious seconds that my wits made an agreement with my mitts. I remembered something my ol' grandpappy taught me called the "Ol' One, Two, Three." It is a classic dwarf brawling technique. Read on and I'll tells ya all about it.

For the first part, I grabbed a fistful of my fine dwarven beard. I marveled at the texture of my face curtain. Part one complete.

Lionheart turned his attention back to his prey, which he thought was me, and looked at me all menacingly.

This is where I shows you part two.

Part two is me shoving a pungent bouquet of dwarf beard right into his big old elfy eyes.

He howled like someone just stabbed rusty needles into his eyeballs, and I can't blame him for screaming neither. Dwarf beards are naturally coarse like a fine barbed wire. Now combine that with all the sweat, booze, bean juice, garlic, onions, and peppers I been marinating my beard in for the last hour or so, and you got yourself a nice little case of . . . Yeah, "rusty needles in the eyeballs" just about sums that up perfectly.

Poor Lionheart flailed around wildly, and it was then that I enacted the climactic part three of the "Ol' One, Two, Three." Well, it really ain't that climactic.

Part three is basically just me sucker booting him in the crotch basket.

My foot sank so far up past his stomach that I felt my toes tickle his spine. With a huge gushing sound, all his wind and wine decided to leave his body in one split second. He fell to the floor in a heap. See, kids, listening pays off. Remember how he was telling us that when his followers forsaked—forsooked . . . yeah, that's right—when the followers forsooked the gods, that they all grew weak? Bor's beard, I was lucky! I bet he used up whatever reserved powers he had been storing up by breaking my practically unbreakable DWoid.

I let him sit there for a moment, gasping and groaning, while I picked up the pieces of my DWoid. Hmphf! Didn't look too bad. I was just starting to put some things together when my brain started doing the same.

Ya know, Grim, said my brain, *I think this place is legit. I mean, who else but someone of godlike strength could break something protected by your powerful rune magic?*

Yeah, maybe you're right, I said to my brain. I mean, the grub and grog alone here were of a supernatural varietal!

Don't get me wrong: gods, goddesses, and divine spirits are all fine and dandy with me, as long as they ain't asking me to contribute to some basket being passed around. Personally, the only divine spirits I tend to rely on are those of the fine dwarven variety, aged in oak barrels. Plus, I always did just right believing in my ol' self.

I was feeling kind of bad now, so I leaned over and helped the Lion to his stool. His elf sidekicks returned back from the kitchen; good thing they weren't around a few seconds ago, as I might have had to try the slightly more elaborate "Ol' One, Two, Three, Four, Five, Six." I'll explain that one to ya another time.

"Now look here, Lionheart. I ain't got nothing to do with no ePhones, elfin technologies, or disestablishment of no heavenly pantheon. This DWoid is 100 percent pure dwarven ingenuity, and it is new to market, so this here has nothing to do with your predicament."

"Bah!" he snarled. "It's all the same. It is that technology that stole away our faithful. It is that sort of device that stole our followers."

He rose up menacingly, and a rumble sounded deep in his chest. The rest of the bar fell in behind him. Now I have shown previously that I can take on *one* weakened god, but I don't know about a whole barroom full of gods! A nonliteral lightning bolt struck my mind, and I had to smile.

"Sooo, is all this maudlin and mopiness about getting *followers*? If'n it's followers you guys are after, I can get you followers. Heh, millions of 'em if you want."

That seemed to perk up the patrons of the bar even more than the brawl that just happened.

"You jest," said Lionheart. "How could someone like you manage something as impossible as that?"

I held up the DWoid he broke, which was now glowing brightly.

Plus one for technology!

INFI.NET POSSIBILITIES

"So how come I can't use my real name?"

I slapped my head in frustration. Gods or not, these guys are techno-stupid! "Because someone else has already taken that name! Why don't you use one of the other suggestions, like 'Lion.Heart' or 'LionHeart114?'"

The god of the hunt growled a curse. "Fine, just pick one for me. I don't care. So this is how we will gain our followers back? Explain to me what this Fae-Book is again."

I calmed myself and proceeded to explain it to him like a parent would to an ignorant god-child.

"Let's start at the basics, okay? First, the Infi.net. Now, the Infi.net is a multi-realm-wide system of interconnected elfin computer networks that link up with billions of other computers in all the realms. The Fae Realm, the mortal realm, and apparently even this here land of the gods. Sounds great and all, but in reality, it's just a big time waster where people go and play games and spend hours upon hours reading articles about movie stars having babies and watch videos, most of which are about kittens. On the Infi.net, there are millions of places you can 'virtually' visit. Places like Crapslist and Sickipedia, the latter where you can look up 'sprained ankle' and find out you might have a brain tumor. And, of course, Fae-Book. Now, Fae-Book is sort of different from regular sites because, for some reason, people feel the need to look at it every other minute or sooner to make sure they aren't missing anything important."

Lionheart looked perplexed. "What things do people do that demand such a constant vigil? Are our ex-followers saving villages from fires or building great shelters to harbor the homeless?"

After about ten minutes, I was able to get my laughter under wraps.

"No, that ain't the point of Fae-Book. The whole reason to go onto Fae-Book is to get as many followers as you can so you can show them all how much better your life is than theirs."

The room was clearly not understanding the words that were coming out of my mouth, so I switched my DWoid to "projector mode." The screen produced a 3-D holo-image of itself that floated in the air above it. I'd like to see an ePhone do that!

"See here." I loaded up a random page of a pretty elf gal, a fe-melf. "So here we have an average elf-ette, riding in a super fancy hovercar and holding her ePhone. She writes, 'My life sucks,' and beneath the picture are over five hundred responses. Here are some samples of what her followers said:

"'I'm so jealous, you suck.'

"'I hate you, tee-hee.'

"'My life suxx more worser.'"

On the last response, there was a photo attached. I was about to click the link when the barroom erupted and started pointing out certain spelling and grammatical errors on the screen.

"Yeah, I know; it's spelled all wrong. That's not important on Fae-Book. Now shush up and pay attention, you grammar god-zis."

I clicked the link, and we saw a male elf, a melf, riding shirtless upon a robotic flying unicorn, and in his dainty hands, he was holding up *two* ePhones.

The picture had over one thousand responses.

Not only that, but look here: between these two elfs, they had over twenty thousand followers!

The gods were all just staring at each other blankly, and Lionheart looked like he ate something that left a turd taste in his mouth.

"How can these two unimportant, grammatically ignorant mortals have the attention of so many followers? Are they all so consumed with paltry matters and image? Did they at least engineer this hovercraft and mechanical unicorn they are glorifying in these images?"

"No, that's not how it works, Lion," I said. "The whole idea is to take things other people have busted their butts creating and present them as your own. People love using quotes they didn't write and showing pictures of food they ain't cooked to represent themselves and their accomplishments."

"Do these mortals create nothing of their own?" cried Lionheart in exasperation.

"Not really. Well, unless you consider *elfies*; then they do," I said to the fallen god.

I don't think I pacified him when I told him what elfies were either. Now in case those at home don't know what I am talking about, allow me to explain. Elfies are self-shot pictures that a person takes of themselves, using one of five classic poses: the "I have fish lips," the "I am surprised," or it could be the "I have cleavage" or the "I have abs." But usually it is the ever-popular "bathroom mirror" sexy pose. Nothing says classy like a photo in the crapper!

"So this is how we are to gain the attention of these empty-headed and self-consumed beings? Explain to me how this Fae-Book will help us when we are stuck *here* and they are out *there*."

After I explained to him about the whole Infi.net thing again, I launched into the details.

"It's simple. You make a profile. Let's call you TheRealLionheart to distinguish you from the fakers out there. Then, let's set up your basic information, like height, weight, where you work. Okay, let's put, 'Currently in between jobs,' and what your religious views are, which would be, 'I worship myself,' I guess. And boom! Your profile is done. Now all we need is a picture of you."

I clicked the DWoid's camera and take a beautiful mugshot of Lionheart and uploaded it to his Fae-Book page.

"Now, all you need to do is start posting stuff that will get the attention of the whole Infi.net. So you would probably say something like . . ."

I looked to Lionheart, waiting for the god of the hunt to dazzle me with some holy words.

He was staring at the screen, looking at his pretty, high-resolution picture that I just took.

"Before we continue, can you retake that picture? There is an odd shadow falling on my forehead that mars my appearance."

I sighed and took another picture. And another one, and on and on. None were up to Lionheart's standards. Finally, in a fit of frustration, I handed him the DWoid and told him to take the blasted picture himself. He held the DWoid as cautiously as if he was holding a dang nether viper. Soon enough he took a picture and nodded in acceptance.

"There, that one looks more fitting. See how I got my hair in the frame, as well as my abs?"

Mortal or immortal, an elf is still an elf.

"Now, Lionheart, what will be the first thing you want to say to your soon-to-be *billions* of new followers?"

Lionheart straightened up, shook his mane, and held his head up majestically. The gods gathered around, and even Donnie Rio and the

Profits of Doom silenced their shredding to hear this most momentous of moments.

The god of the hunt opened his mouth and proudly said—

"*You still sitting in my chair!*"

I slapped my head for about the hundredth time tonight, ready to put to rest the bloated troll god of annoyance. I wheeled around, hand hammers cocked and loaded, to stand once again mug-to-gut with Glubb'gar . . . and now, his mates. I just thought he was talking about his friends, you know, his *mates*, his bros, his buddies. What I saw was Glubb'gar standing center stage with about six of the fugliest, most monstrous troll "ladies" these peepers have ever had the horror to see.

"So, uhh, these are your mates?" I said, politely.

He punched his fat palm with a greasy fist. "Well, we friends. Nothing too serious."

The gods began to clear out of the area, sensing the brawl that was percolating, all except Lionheart and his elfs. They stood by my side. Isn't this a weird story? As you know, on the outside, elfs and dwarves are enemies, but here, at God's End, things are different.

DON'T FEED THE TROLLS

So this whole evening had to be the strangest night of my already colorful existence. Here I was, standing side by side with the elfin gods whose futuristic-al ex-followers all want me dead. *And* we were up against the gods of the trolls, who also wanted me dead, or at least smashed up a bit. I grabbed the chair that I been sitting on and placed it in front of me.

"All right, moss-brains, you want this chair? Well, boy-o, come and get it! Yeah, bring your lady friends. You'll need some real muscle to take me on."

Glubb'gar tossed a pig hoof he was chewing on and started licking his thick fingers.

"Narp, my mates are for the elflings. They think elfs cute, and I say they can keep if they can catch."

The ladies swooned as a look of horror passed over the elfs. With a scream, the troll-ettes charged them, and you have never seen anyone, or anything, scatter so fast. Glubb'gar turned to me and laughed.

"Me and little beard have unfinished fight ahead of us. Now time for you to get smashed."

I flipped out of the way as a giant greasy hand came crashing down. I grabbed the chair and hurled it at Glubb'gar, and it smashed into his glorious gut. Enraged, he lunged at me, and I maneuvered left as I sunk a right into his belly, but he just blinked like something got in his eye. Whether it was his divine being-ness or the abundant rolls of troll fat that dampened my blow, I don't know. He managed to wrap me up in a wrassler's hold, but what with all them greasy swine products he had been devouring all day, I slipped out of his bear hug like a, well, like a greased pig!

Now the band started to pick up, seeing that they had a nice "pit" going round and round the dance floor. The music was great, as it is rare to have a soundtrack accompany a good ol' dwarven beatdown, played by no less than the band of the gods!

The elfs didn't know what to do. In a normal fracas, I bet Lionheart and his crew of primal elfs would have laid into their foes with all sorts of ferociousness, but since their foes were hoe—uhh—were of the feminine persuasion, they couldn't really do anything but block and parry the meaty hands and slobbering kisses. While dodging one hammy haunch, Lionheart accidentally smacked another patron, a red-bearded, hammer-wielding barbarian. The barbarian roared in anger as his drinking horn crashed to the ground.

"Thou hast broketh mine drinking horn! Thou-est wilst pay-eth for such-eth an insult!" He whirled his hammer around and hurled it mightily. With the reflexes of a shadow panther, Lionheart managed to avoid the flying mallet, but the troll gal who was groping for him didn't, and the hammer hit her with a crack of thunder that laid her flat. The hammer ricocheted off the troll and went soaring into the bar.

The red-bearded guy rushed over to the fallen troll-ette, who was clearly counting stars. "M'lady, a thousand pardons. I meant—"

He soon joined her in calculating astronomy as the flat edge of a mighty sword was slammed down on his winged-helmed head. This knightly looking guy, in white, shining armor, strode forward and held his hand out to the troll, who was now coming to after that little tap to the dome.

"I have protected and redeemed your honor, fair maid—" The white knight was dropped an instant later when the barbarian's hammer, still flying around looking for its keeper, smashed him in his mug. He stumbled back and crashed into a table and was then slugged by a giant tree dude who had been disturbed while drinking his glass of rain. The tree guy accidentally bumped into an eight-armed, scimitar-wielding goddess, and she took to pruning the poor sap. (Get it? Tree guy? Sap? Bah, never mind!)

Fights now broke out everywhere, and the whole joint seemed to be squabbling furiously, the event looking more like a dang prison riot than a bar fight! Some of the patrons doing battle even stumbled into Grandma's kitchen, and they quickly stumbled out, sporting a variety of meat thermometers and serving forks stuck in their hides.

I was so distracted watching the mayhem that I forgot all about Glubb'gar! I looked over, and he was busy, not eating but wiping off his hands with some hot towels he had found at a serving station. He moved in; and I laid another couple of body blows that would have felled an aurochs but didn't do nothing but tickle him. (Sorry, aurochs are big old bisony-looking beasts that are now extinct. I should just stick with the simple vocabularies like cow or bovine, as I know I have a lot of humans reading these here yarns.) So anyway, Glubb'gar fetched me up, and unlike the last time, now I was trapped!

"Hands all clean! Now me dirty them up again with dwarf juice."

He held me fast and headbutted me a time or two, smashed me into the floor, the wall, and so on, but I didn't feel nothing. As we know, trolls hit like stone, but dwarfs are made of iron! I have to admit, though, that after a few minutes of this mash-up, my iron was starting to dent a little bit.

Naturally I fought back, but my attacks did nothing but get stuck in rolls of nasty neck, belly, and chin fat. His pummeling was shaking me rather fierce, and I heard something jingle and go clinkity-clink on the floor.

I thought maybe I dropped my DWoid, so during the flogging I started checking my pockets for it. I didn't find my DWoid; it was on the table, showing off Lionheart's new Fae-Book page.

After groping myself, I finally figured out what dropped out of my pockets. It was then that my genius-ness contacted me and let me know what to do to get out of my current predicament. Since violence ain't solving my problem, I decided to go with some less hostile stra-tegery. I began poking under Glubb'gar's arms and chin. He started giggling, so I really got to burrowing in.

"Ha! What you—hah ha ha—doing?" chuckled the big troll.

I ignored him and tickled the sides of his belly, which caused Glubb'gar to roar, not in pain or anger but in laughter. He dropped me, and I charged in with a series of right and left tickles of terror, each finding a home in neck rolls and gelatinous side belly. The troll guffawed like a donkey and backed up, trying to avoid my assault. What my fists of fury couldn't achieve, my fingers of funny did.

It was then that I enacted the finale of this episode. From my pocket, I withdrew the round glass stones that made up the shore of the island of fallen gods, and I threw them across the floor at Glubb'gar.

They skittered across the linoleum tile like butter on a hot griddle. Glubb'gar rubbed his sides and shook off the smile that was on his face.

"All right, little dwarfling. Time to stop laughing and start crying," he said as he stepped forward. He immediately set foot on the stones and started flailing like a flatulent palm tree in a tsunami. He spun around and around and finally came down with a crash that shook the joint. He tried to get up again and, just as swiftly, fell down.

Pretty soon all the brawling gods stopped their fighting to watch the evening's comedic showcase. Hilarity ensued, and even Glubb'gar's mates were having a laugh. I was suddenly feeling a bit sad. I mean, I know he wanted to smash me and kill me to pieces, but I just wanted to get away; I didn't want to humiliate the poor lummox.

I moved forward to help out the big guy, and, wouldn't you know it, I stepped onto some of the dang stones too! Now I was spinning around like a bearded tornado, and I realized I was flailing face-first into what looked like a big window overlooking the ocean. I lashed out at anything that could help steady me. I managed to clasp onto my crate of DWoids, but even that wasn't heavy enough to stop my trajectory toward the glass. I smashed through the window and found myself falling three or four stories down to the ocean below.

I didn't recall going up no stairs in this weird, god-infested tavern! Bor's beard, I still didn't know how I even got there! I had just enough time to guzzle one last gulp of air before I splashed into the blue drink below.

HERE TODAY, GOD TOMORROW

The cold water hit me like that silly "Ice Bucket Challenge" all these attention seekers are doing on the Infi.net.

I was not in the water for more than a second or two, but it took me a split second to deduce that what I was wallowing in was good ol' fashioned saltwater.

Then I was catapulted upwards and landed like a bearded fish upon the deck of the *Ol' Girl*. She gave me a lick with her big ol' forked tongue, and I looked around confusedly.

"Where in Bor's bungled brain am I?" I shouted to my crew, who was busy returning fire at an elfin Centaur-class battlecruiser.

Bjorn chimed in after he let loose with a barrage from his two laz guns that he was somehow blasting away with:

"Captain fall off ship"—*blam, blam, blam*—"and get brained by crates. *Ol' Girl* swoops down"—*blam, blam, blam*—"and fishes Captain up again!"

Mon'Goro was busy deflecting laser blasts with his blade and sipping the remnants of his smoothie that didn't end up spilled on the deck. He leaned over and touched the back of my head.

"The blazes, Mongo! What are you doing?" I cried as I ducked behind his purple bulk, trying to avoid the heavy cannon fire.

"It appears you have a rather large bump on your head, my dear Captain. Let me take a look at that—well, after we tidy up this little mess we have gotten ourselves into. Can you hold this?" he asked, handing me the empty shake cup.

Mon'Goro grabbed Bjorn and charged into the fray. The *Ol' Girl* got in good and close, and like a damn grape ballerina with a blade, Mongo leapt in the air and cut a small helmet-sized hole in the hull of the battlecruiser.

"I sink battleship now?" said Bjorn, almost politely, to Mongo.

"I believe it is time, Assistant to the Captain Bjorn," says Mon'Goro, and he expertly dunked Bjorn into the ship's breach.

"That be *Assistant Captain*, ya dumb cook," he said as he disappeared into the hull.

I heard a bunch of screams and explosions as Bjorn tore apart the insides of the battleship, but I don't want to bore you with all that. Let's get back to the hero of the story: me!

So I was sitting there, thinking, *Was this all in my head? Am I going nuts?*

I felt the back of my head, and it seemed like I was growing a dang dragon egg there. My hat was pitching up like a tent!

Laser blasts started hitting around my general vicinity, so I dove behind my DWoid crate. A brilliant green laser hit it dead center and proceeded to destroy my cover.

I smelled a really pungent smell, and my eyes started to tear up. Now I was downright pissed!

"Okay, not only am I going crazy, but now I was crying?"

I looked around and saw the remnants of the crate, and as it turns out, I grabbed the wrong box when I was trying to save myself from falling out the barroom window.

Mon'Goro came a-running back to see if I was okay, and he sniffed the air hungrily.

"Honorable Captain, what is that beautiful aroma?" he said as he helped me up.

On the deck were the last vestiges of the crate, and among the ruins, rightly sizzled from laser fire, was a bunch of onions, garlic, and red peppers.

Huh, I guess that meant I left my DWoids at the bar. No big deal; I have plenty more where they came from. Plus, I have no clue how to get back to where I was, since I don't even know how I got there in the first place.

Mon'Goro was salivating like the *Ol' Girl* at chow time, and he gathered all the vegetables that was strewn about the deck in his apron. "Ahhhh, this scent is truly from the realm of the gods!"

I took a deep whiff.

"That's downright possible, Mongo, but to me, it just smells like Grandma's kitchen."

I adjusted my hat and boarded my new elfin battlecruiser.

EPILOGUE

So there ya have it. This story clearly demonstrates some examples of technology being an aid or a downright hindrance to my hide. In the end, I think the pluses vs. minuses ended up in a tie. Either way, technology is pretty fantastic; it's just the folks who can't disconnect from it that drive me nuts.

After the battle, me and the crew combed the waters for any signs of the entrance to the God's End Tavern, but we never could find it. Bjorn even offered to smash some DWoid crates over my head to see if that would send me back there, but I decided I didn't want to find it that bad.

Besides, if I ever want to visit, I can just go online. Oh yeah, Lionheart, Glubb'gar, and all the other deities at the God's End are on Fae-Book now and gathering up followers like you wouldn't believe! Lionheart hosts an outdoor survival show, a DWoid-cast called Trapped on an Island, which is pretty popular with the doomsday enthusiasts. It's nothing fancy, but most tend to like it.

And everyone loves Glubb'gar! I mean, he's a giant celebrity now. Constantly in verbal battles with people, talking smack and telling them he will destroy them or that they are awful singers. He is widely known as the first troll on the Infi.net, and unlike most Infi.net posters, who talk like they is ten feet tall and able to whoop your ass, Glubb'gar is and can!

The *Ol' Girl* and Cer-Ber-Rus (that is the username of Cerci, Bertrum, and Rusty) send each other kitty vids back and forth and are set to go on a playdate, should we ever discover how to get back to the land of the gods.

Can you believe that even Grandma has a Fae-Book page? She and Mon'Goro have a nice little recipe-trading thing going on with each other, and I tell ya, I haven't ate better, excepting for the grub served from Grandma's kitchen.

Maybe I'll get back there one day, but until then, I guess I'll just have to be content to listen to Donnie Rio and the Profits of Doom on my DWoid. You won't hear them on eTunes, though, as they signed an exclusive agreement with Grim's Hymns. *Live at God's End* is set to sell over one million copies! Pretty good numbers, considering all the inconsiderate music piracy that goes on these days!

The End

GRIMBEARD

GOES FISHING

You ever have a friend who hooks up with someone who is completely wrong for them? They changes their attitude and even the way they dress, all over a piece of tail . . . Ha boyo, that is funny! Well, you will understand why it's so funny once you start reading the story. This whole situation just happened to my Assistant to the Captain, Bjorn Huge. Seems weird that someone as independent could become so dang dependent! And all it took was a song, a bat of an eye, and a kiss. That's all it took to hook him. She wasn't even that great, to tell you the truth. I've seen him with better but never has I seen him with worse. Anyway, this here is a whale of a tale about tail and as anything, it starts out easily enough. It started with me going fishing.

MO-MOS ARE NO-NOS

I woke up well before ol' Bright Eye (that's what I calls the sun) was even blinking above the horizon of this Rock, which is what I call this here world we sail on. Technically, I guess I never woke up, per say, as I never fell asleep yet from the night before. Me and my crew of two—Assistant to the Captain Bjorn Huge and my cook, Mon'Goro, fell into a few barrels of recently liberated mo-mo wine we had procured from an elfin cargo ship. This vessel was a "small catch" as we fishing enthusiasts like to say, and like all small catches, you should toss them back so they can get good and fat when they grows up or, in this case, restocks their supplies. The elfin crew seemed more than happy to let us have what goods they had since I promised not to send them down into the briny blue all a'smoldering, but I was a bit miffed that their cargo was just cask after cask of the aforementioned despicably, stickily, sickly sweet fermented fruit piss. So I was fuming red, but Mon'Goro was all aglow in various shades o' purple at obtaining what he called the "elixir of tranquility." Well, this elixir is anything but tranquil on my innards, as mo-mos makes me chum the waters from both bow and stern if'n you get my meaning. Now I can already hear my overly concerned readers out there yammering about my health.

"Well, Grimbeard, why did you drink the mo-mo juice if you don't like it and you know it doesn't agree with your body? Why would you do that to yourself? Maybe you have a drinking pro—"

Let me butt in, as I think I gets the gist of what you all are yapping on about. Why do I imbibe something I dislikes and that I know is bad on my guts? Well, why I drinks something that ain't particularly fond of me is because . . . Ya see, it's the same thing as, well, I guess why someone would want to eat nasty gas-station pizza. Now, no self-respecting gastronomican would consume such a frightening, unpalatable piece of greasy cardboard, dried ketchup, and the wood shavings that they pass off as cheese. BUT, if'n someone hands you a couple of free pies of them GSPs, well, you might change your view, ya know? I mean, after all, it's free and no matter how bad it is, it's still pizza, right? So mo-mo wine and other aperitifs is a lot like gas-station pizzas . . . and french fries, chocolate, and sex. Even the bad stuff is still pretty good. Well, I can't expect you all to understand my advanced thought processes, so how's about I get back to this here yarn I am trying to spin?

As I was saying, I was a bit shipwrecked from the night before, and I decided to let ol' Bjorn sleep in a bit, me being a concerned captain and all. He ain't much the drinker since he is only a head after all. I don't know how he even gets half-crocked what with all the mo-mo wine dribbling out his neck hole, but he sure is a lightweight. Mongo, the once-dreaded warlord of the wastes turned culinary disciple, was up as well, looking no worse for wear. I said good-bye to him but he had his ear buds jammed in deep and was ensorcelled by the glowing screen of his DWoid. Mongo was just finishing up an episode of Prawn Stars and started up on some weird fish talk show, I think it's called the Moray Show. I ain't got no clue as to what that show is about, but every time I watches it, some slick-looking eel with a pompadour is telling some skinny piece of white fish that he is or is not the dad of some weird-looking kid with a giant humpback whale-of-a-gal mom. Then everyone gets into a fight and Moray thanks them. Pretty entertaining, actually! Well, as I was saying, even my superior constitution was feeling a bit low at the moment, so I administered a tried-and-true remedy

to reinvigorate mind, body, and spirit. After a few barrels of suds (to rehydrate myself after a night of delicate destruction), I grabbed my rod, and—no, I don't mean that one, I mean my ol' fishin' pole—and headed overboard in my little life raft. Nothing cures almost-hangovers and irritable *bow* syndrome better than a morning of leisurely, back-breaking rowing and casting some lines into the drink. So with oars in my mitts, I hunkered over, bent wood-to-wave, and headed off to start what seemed to be a nice, restful day. Oh boyo, was I wrong.

SOMETHING FISHY THIS WAY COMES

So I set off and was rowing away to this peach of a spot—ugh, peaches kinda reminds me of mo-mos. Let's say, I was rowing to a beaut of a spot that I knows about that was only a few leagues from where the *Ol' Girl* sat hovering a hundred feet off the ocean's surface. Yeah, my ship flies, but I ain't got time to reiterate information I done explained already in nearly every other tale I've told! If you ain't understanding the words that are coming out of my mouth, you is uneducated and should immediately get rightly schooled up by reading "Grimbeard Goes to Prison," which is included in this here collection of tales! That one will tell ya all the info you are delinquent on, so stop skipping ahead to the previous stories!

Now, like I was saying before I interrupted myself, I was rowing away, and the leagues disappeared just like my need to hurl my guts out, and by the time I found my fishing spot, I felt good as new. I cast in my line and basked in the pre-dawn quietness of the moment; it was just me, the salty air, and the wee sharks nibbling away at my keel. Then all of the sudden, the salty winds started to blow all saccharine on me, and I heard this gods-awful tune start drifting in off the waves, invading my solitude. Lyrically it was nothing to write home about and went something like:

"Ahoy there young sailor, how's about a date, bend to my will and seals your fate . . ."

The melody was trying its darnedest to be catchy, and it had a distinct (and I mean heavy on the "stink") whiff of elfin pop music. It sounded like someone was trying to imitate that fat elfin pop star, Adelf. Ah, I shouldn't be so harsh on her as "fat," for an elf clocks in at about a hundred pounds (and that is considered morbidly obese).

Now I loves me some good nautical tunes, but this weren't floating my dingy, and blast it if the caterwauling didn't start to scare away all the big shark-fishes! Well, technically they wasn't really swimming away, more accurately they was swimming *toward* the mewling. I glanced over in the general vicinity of the caterwauling and saw a slinky, feminine-ish figure sitting on a rock jutting out of the water, and she was just combing away at her long blue-green tresses, singing her wannabe effin' elfin pop poop, and staring right at me all coy-like. She looked to be about eight feet long, yeah I mean *long*, as her lower torso looked like that of a dang fish! I checked out her upper deck, and sure enough it was all dolled-up like a bona fide elfin pop star but with added fish bits like gills, scales, and fins.

Since my sweet spot turned to a sour patch, I let go of the small sharks I'd caught and started rowing back toward the *Ol' Girl*, grumbling about how my mission o' fishing ended too soon. As I was paddling back, this fish bi—, ahem, this female, was singing even louder than before, trying to beckon me over to her, all the while combing her hair and batting her big ol' fish eyes at me. Fuming, I breezed right by her without another glance. I likes my wimmens more curvy and a lot less fishy smelling. It seems like sharks ain't as aurally or olfactory-ily discerning as I am, as her song whirled them up something right fierce, and they started to chomp and grab at her. Some of them even leapt out of the water, and what do you know, they wasn't just sharks, but they was a bunch of shark men!

"By the sea gods, help me, sailor!"

Thankfully she stopped the singing, and I started looking for this sailor she was yapping at. I mean, I didn't see no sailors, I just saw me, but I ain't no mere sailor—I'm a dang captain!

She went on and on for a spell, with all sorts of shrieks that I managed to shut out by singing to myself a real nautical song that I composed meself about the best dang captain ever to sail water or air!

"Oh, who is the roughest, the gruffest, the toughest, captain on land, air, or sea?"

"Listen up landling! I command you to help me!" she shouted out, trying to mess up my beautiful little chanty I was singing. I forgot how much I love my theme song, and I don't do so well with being ordered around, so I really started belting out the tunes with some pepper!

"Who is fighting-est, drinking-all-nighty-est? Put up your dukes and you'll see."

"Very well, if my songs can't capture your heart, maybe I can offer you the queen's booty," she said all alluringly, shaking her scaly hips. Do fish even have hips? Anyway, I am more about goods than services and I kept on keeping on.

"Who is purtiest, dirtiest, courteous, scoundrel of pure dignity?"

"Then how about the royal treasure ches—," she lost any ounce of previous alluringness when she was jounced by a hammer-headed-man-shark dude trying to get fresh with her. She lashed out with her big ol' tail and sent him flying off the rock just as I finished my song up with a triumphant roar.

"Who robs from the elfs and gives to himselfs, Captain Grimbeard is he. Oh, Captain Grimbeard is me!"

"Ooooooh, blast you to the seven blue hells, I am rich and I have money!"

Just then, my chivalrous nature got the best of me. I mean, there was a female in trouble and it was my duty to procure—uhh, protect—that damsel's hide! I spun my boat and high-sailed it toward the fish woman. Hitting rock, I leapt from the boat, oar in hand, and plowed into the shark-men surrounding her all hungrily.

This must all sound funny to you land folks, shark men, fish wimmens, and the like, but out here, we sees all kinds of weirdos from unda-da-sea. (I probably shouldn't be so liberal with the use of the sea-word. I know a particular company out there that can become very litigious with their intellectual properties; I thinks I will retract and rephrase the previous sentence to something like, "We sees all kinds of weirdos from unda-da-ocean.")

Now back to the story with no more commercial interruptions.

As I was saying, there was this school of shark gents and they was just about to get teached by professor Grimbeard and his six-foot-long ruler. I waded in (pun intended) and—Bor's briny barnacles!—it looked like I was hosting Shark Week, except there weren't no hi-def plasma screen between me and them chomping teeth! Class soon started, and after a few minutes of my curriculum, I sent the shark dudes home early to get started on their homework, mostly reading up on how to fix bent gills, busted fins, and broken teeth. I turned to the lady and addressed her with all courtesy and manners: "Hello there, the name's Grimbeard, now where is the money you *oomph.*—"

The woman pounced on me and she seemed more like half octopus than half fish! I fought her off, but not before she almost smooched my whiskers!

"Easy, easy, now! I rescue you from that group of fins with teeth and you repay with this mugging! That ain't no way for a lady—well, half a lady—to be acting!"

She looked at me in wonder and then her eyes blinked in amazement.

"You astonishingly resist my arias and you, you, you . . . rebuff my queenly adorations!" Tears appeared in her big ol' fish eyes and her gills started to quiver. "You really wish to have something as insignificant as money instead of *this*?" she said, pointing to herself as she broke down and started with the waterworks. I patted her on her dorsal fin.

"Now, now, it don't have to be money . . . come on . . . how about gems? Gold coins or the like? It all spends the same," I answered back with all courtesy. Just then I heard a roar and an incredible *whoosh* over my head, nearly blowing my captain's hat off my noble dome. I spun around, raising my fists and oar, thinking the shark men had come back to turn in their homework. Nope, unfortunately school was out for the day and it was . . . well, read on. It starts getting good now!

THE BIRDS AND THE BEES
AND UNDA-DA-SEAS

The *whoosh* was soon followed by a loud draconic barking, and I saw my ship, the *Ol' Girl*, flying down. She sat her ol' bones in the water next to me, which nearly capsized me, but due to my expert captaining of any vessel I sets my keister on, I kept my rowboat afloat. I started scratching her keel, and she brought her big ol' noggin' down and gave me a lick.

"Dijoo you miss me, girl? Huh? Dijoo come looking for daddy?" I said in the voice we all uses when talking to doggies. She shook her head and nodded back to a clanging sound coming from the deck.

"Bjorn Huge hear most pretty song calling to him, telling Bjorn to come!" bounced the aforementioned Bjorn Huge off the deck. He landed with a loud clank and was staring up at the mer-lady like Mongo stares at his dang DWoid screen. Speaking of Mongo, I saw his purple melon pop over the poop and look down at us all astonished-like.

"Qu—, Que—," was all he kept stuttering out, so I chucked a rock or two at him to help him clear out whatever he was trying to say, but he deftly sent them flying back at me, causing me to duck lest I got brained.

"Speak up, Mongo; you got plop-corn stuck in your throat again?"

Mon'Goro leapt off the deck of the *Ol' Girl* and landed like an elfin gymnast on the slick, wet rocks. He popped out his earbuds and bowed with a flourish.

"Greetings, most honorable Queen Sireen. I am so glad to see you safe, sound, and happily found," he said all reverentially.

"Of course she is safe," I blurted out. "I done run off some sea-thugs that was getting all uppity on her, and we was just talking about the payment method of my reward." I turned back to her, patting her scaly back and recapped that money, i.e., gems, gold coins, etc., were all valid forms of payment for the heroic services rendered.

Mon'Goro shook his bushy-bearded head and proceeded to remove a rolled-up magazine from his chef's apron. "Look here, my good captain, the queen has been missing for months," he said, tapping the cover with a thick purple finger.

I took a gander and, sure enough, there was an awful picture of our girl, right on the front page, hanging out with what appeared to be variety of unsavory-looking mer-folk. It always bristles my beard, I mean, the queen weren't no looker in my opinion, what being half fish and all, but why do them dang magazine editors always pick the ugliest picture possible of us? We gots our eyes half-closed and our mouth in mid-drool. It's like they is, on purpose, trying to make us look bad! Anyway, above and beneath the fugly image, it was all emblazoned with words like "wild weekends," "unqueenly behavior," and "Fathom furious and finished!"

Fathom? As in King Fathom? I started to get a sick feeling in my stomach and it had nothing to do with no mo-mos. I flipped through the magazine and sure as shi—uh . . . shitake mushrooms, there was a pic of our girl in a wedding dress, looking a lot less worn out, standing next to a gia-gantic-ly muscled, green-bearded dude holding a golden trident. That was King Fathom all right.

I started to sweat a bit more than I normally do, as King Fathom and I have some history between us that stems directly from bad luck and a bad pick down at the ol' sea-horse track. See, I knew Fathom when he was the bachelor king and we was doing what bachelors do: drink, have fun, gamble, and not have to deal with trivial filial obligations. So we was hanging out at the track with some of his guardsmen, and after a few bad picks, ol' Fathom was running a bit short on *clams* (that's unda-da-ocean slang for cash). He and I chatted about financial matters and I was kind enough to lend him some clammies, and in exchange, he'd let me hold on to his golden trident as collateral till his horse won. Well, not to bore you with the details, but his sea horse of course lost, and I ended up with his ol' trident.

Oh, and one other tiny thing, Fathom sorta caught me in the bait shack with his sister; that also might have something to do with his immense hatred of me. He said I "sullied the royal lineage of the Fathom name with my grubby, landlubber-y fingers," but I told him I never even touched her with my fingers. That really bent his flippers, and I barely made it out of the dang ocean before he and his squad of mermaid-men nabbed me.

I still had the old trident, and I didn't even use it for anything, though I think Mongo used it for cooking plop-dogs when he went camping. *Maybe I should bring it with me?* I thought. He is a pretty powerful king now, so I figured he has some coinage to pay back past debts. On second thought, if this here woman was Fathom's missing wife, hell, his *queen*, then I should just gets as far away as possible; he probably would think that I been "lubbering" with his woman, and in most cases I know, husbands love their wives more than their sisters, and in some places unda-da-ocean, they is the same person! I adjusted my hat and made a captainly decision.

"Alrighty, boys, we needs to get a'moving," I was about to hands Mongo back his rag mag when the queen snatched it mid-pass.

"Oh, I love seeing myself in magazines, I—oh, that's not my best picture now, is it." She giggled and started shuffling through the pages, reminiscing at all her glory days gone by, and I saw her smile turn upside down when her peepers landed on an image of Fathom standing next to a really unattractive fish-faced-female. The queen's eyes narrowed and she started reading to herself. I couldn't hear exactly what she was saying, me trying not to pry and all, but I could make out a few words that sounded like "royal flush" and "separates" and "finds new love." The more she read, the more venom coated her words. She crumpled up the tabloid and removed a small device that looked like a scallop shell. I recognized it immediately as a cheap unda-da-ocean imitation of a DWoid, some nautical knock-off called a shellPhone. She deftly input some digits with a webbed hand and made a call. Someone picked up, and I heard her start tearing into the party on the other end, saying things like "child support" and "spousal support," and even something about "taking someone on a trip to the cleaners." She hung up by smashing the shellPhone on the rocks below and proceeded to scream at the top of her gills. Her fins flared up, and her tail started lashing around, and just when I thought she was going to explode with all this very unqueenly behavior, Bjorn bounced over to her and started acting all weird. He was acting almost . . . empathical?

"What is it, my beautiful little queen? It okay, Bjorn take care of any problem you have," he said just as sweetly as a disembodied head in a helmet can convey sympathy. Then I saw a miraculous metamorphosis wash over the queen: The flared fins smoothed out, and this gal went from furious to felicitous in a second. Her eyes batted and fluttered, and she picked up Bjorn and cradled him in her arms.

"Oh, my little champion, nothing is wrong at all. Why, I was just invited to a welcome-home party, and I was asked if I knew any strong and handsome individuals that would like to come with me, but silly me, I am lost! So if you aren't too busy, would you want to help me with one, itsy-bitsy, teensy, weensy thing? Will you escort me home to my little welcome-home party?" she asked in a singsongy way. Bjorn started bouncing around in her arms.

"You bet! Bjorn help new girlfriend with anything she need! Bjorn crush, maim, destroy, and even go to stupid party," he said all excitedly.

She smiled all lovingly. "Oh, I don't think it will come to the former, at least, not just yet, anyway. Thank you, my dear. It is so wonderful of you and your crew to return me home." I nearly fell off my boat at the insult.

"*His* crew? First off, hims and thems be *my* crew! And next, ain't no way we is going nowhere with the likes of you. You are obviously having some domestical issues going on and you just so happens to be hitched to someone who wants to separate my neck from my beard." I started hoisting my rowboat back up to the *Ol' Girl*'s deck and got her ready to make like a bakery truck and leave. Bjorn didn't seem to like that idea of leaving his new lady and figuratively jumped up on his desk to say his "Oh captain, my captain."

"Bjorn stay with new girlfriend! Bjorn in love! Captain can go back to fishing for fishies and Bjorn stay with Sireen!" he shouted romantically.

So you think Bjorn's expression of his feelings would make this woman happy, right? Here she had a good, upstanding-ish–type guy cutting out his heart and giving it to her, no strings attached, but no, some people ya can never satisfy or gratify. They keeps looking at the rugged captain, longing for the one that got away . . . to go fishing. She was good though and continued on with the theatrical display of thespianism.

"But if you leave now, how will I return home? Who will protect me? And . . . who will claim the million-dollar reward for my return?"

"I will," said Bjorn and I at the same time, though I think we was both answering different questions. We both look at each other. "You will what?" we said together again, getting in each other's grills. Queen Sireen got right excited as it looked like she was going to get to watch two best-ish friends fight duel for her admirations. Over her shoulder, a purple hand appeared, holding a greasy bag loaded with grayish-pinkish bits.

"Oooh, this is just like the Moray show! Plop-corn?" said Mon'Goro with a toothy grin. After she politely declines, Mongo and the queen return their attention to the sideshow.

"Sireen all mine! You go find own queen!" shouted Bjorn. Now I wasn't going to mention that it ain't polite to yell and gives orders at your captain, but Bjorn weren't in his right head at that moment, being all whammied by his emotions. I decided to talk straight and true to my Assistant to the Captain, like his friend and not his senior ranking officer.

"Bjorn, you are absolutely right," I said with pure dignity.

"What?" said Bjorn and Sireen at the same time. I put my arms around them both and gave them an affirming hug.

"I'll tell you what Bjorny. Obviously you two are good together. And me, being an honorable captain and friend, would never wants to get in the middle of a fine example of true love like we got here. Bjorn, you can have Sireen all to yourself. And me, I guess I'll just have to settle on that little bit of reward money being offered for the queen's safe return as a consolation prize." I patted him on his helmet and turned to the queen apologetically. "Oh, and one more thing, what with all these romantical gestures flying around, please don't forget about the previous discussions on money, i.e., gems, gold coins, etc., that you owe me for past rescuing."

Bjorn cozied up and looked longingly at Queen Sireen, who looked longingly at me, and poor Mon'Goro looked longingly right dejected as the show he just started watching got canceled before the first episode even finished. He tossed his plop-corn down, thought about it, and then started eating off the ground.

"What will you do about King Fathom?"

"Oh, come on, Mongo, you know I'd never let something as simple as someone wanting me dead stand in the way of true love . . . or reward money!"

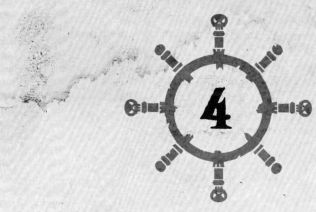

SUITS ME JUST FINE

So the four of us was standing in the middle of the sea and contemplating how we would travels unda-da-ocean to get the reward money—oh, and of course, get the queen (and her new pawn) to the castle (and not get jumped by the king). As I was ruminating my plans, the queen chirped in, acting like she was running the show, and started telling us to lines up. Of course, Bjorn snapped to it and got in front shouting "number one!" and "first post!" or some other nonsense, while Mongo and I stayed put. The queen eyed us threateningly as she picked up Bjorn.

"Now my little knight, I bestow upon thee the 'kiss of the depths.' With this kiss you will be able to breathe under water, and your body will be immune to the effects of water pressure, hypothermia, the bends, and other trivial matters you land mongrels experience below." She then planted a big ol' fish-lipped kiss right on his helmet. (Now gets your brains out of the brine, people, Bjorn is a disembodied head, so when I says his helmet, I means his *helmet*! Come on kids, let's keep those thoughts "above sea-level.") I swears I could see little hearts floating up off of Bjorn after his kiss; it was sad to see them pop when the Queen reached to me hungrily like a last dwarf does a cold mug of suds.

"Now come here and get your kisses." Mongo gave a deep bow and waved his hands apologetically.

"Most humble thanks my queen, but your glorious gift would be wasted on the likes of me. I have trained in the arts of combat and discipline for many hundreds of years and honed my abilities to control my body and focus. I—"

"Fine, I don't care for grape anyway, come along or not," said the queen with a toss of her green locks and a little laugh. Mongo, ever the master of control (except when he goes berserk), nodded and whispered to me.

"I will simply hold my breath for the journey, it won't be more than a day or so."

"Let's hope it don't even take more than an hour; she gives me the dang—ARGH!"

The queen done crept up on my like a sea ghost. "Think of it, little captain, all that reward money sitting down in my palace, and all you need to do is take me there. And the only way to get down unda-da-ocean is to accept my kiss. If you don't, then you can kiss the reward and the money, i.e., gems, gold coins, etc., goodbye."

I started laughing quietly at first but then with a bit more gusto. "So you think that the only way for me to go unda-da-sea is to let you kiss me? Really? Oh Queeny, you must not know me very well." I said through my guffaws. I tapped Mongo. "Does the queen here know me very well?"

"No, Captain, I do not believe she does, as she just met you moments ago," he said, totally not getting the humor of my meaning. The queen was looking right offended and started to get royally indignant at me.

"Well, Mister Captain, why don't you explain to me how you propose to get me home then? I don't recall you being able to breathe underwater," she taunted all imperialistically.

"Give me one second, I needs to go get on my swimming trunks!" I said, and with a bound, I was off to my captain's quarters for a wardrobe change. A few moments later, I came out in my swimmin' suit and proudly announced to my crew and my rescuee, "Okay, I am ready. Now where in Bor's bloody beard are we a'taking you to?"

I was greeted by what sounded like comedy night at a hyena den. Queen Sireen and Bjorn were yucking it up, and even Mongo chuckled enough to start choking on a piece of plop-corn. The only one who had my back was the *Ol' Girl*. She was just barking away and—hey, you don't think dogs just substitute barking because they can't laugh, do ya?

Now, I realizes I ain't the best-looking dwarf in the world—well, actually, I am, since I am the only one left. So let me says, I realizes, I *am* the best-looking dwarf in the world, so I don't know why they would be laughing at me. Maybe it was my new swimmin' suit? I don't think that could be it, as it is a dang marvel of dwarfen engineering! Sure, I coulda bought one of them fancy, high-priced, sparkly, elfish wet suits they have at the mall, but hell, thems are cheaply made and built for individuals who have the body of a seven-year-old malnourished child! I'm a bit stouter than your average elf as you know, and I figured I could saves some money and make one that would accommodate the frame of a real sea-diving man (or dwarf)—one that don't disintegrate once it hits salt water. This here suit is a perfect blend of rune magic and solid dwarfen craftsmanship, so you just know it looks boss! I won't go into details of how badass the suit looks, as the wonderful illustrator of my yarns will do a fine job of it (he better for the amount of coin and ale he leeches from me to do these scribbles). So I let the cackling die down and waited for everyone to wipes the tears from their faces. Okay, now we can continues with our story.

ROYAL CASTLE CRASHERS

So with everyone in tow, we submerged ourselves into the briny blue and started our quest. Bor's bubbles, I forgot how dull it is unda-da-ocean. Top part is good and the bottom is good, but all the rest in the middle is just a bunch of boring, blue nothing. Sure, there is some fishes meandering about, but that is really it.

And the worst part of the journey was having to listen to Queen Sireen's singing. She was yodeling away, and for some reason it seemed to get us a lot of attention. At least three or four times on our way down, we was accosted by hordes of mer-kin, which is just the general name given to underwater denizens like the shark dudes from earlier. It wasn't really a problem, though, as Bjorn was right up front to deal with the troublemakers. Those squabbles was few and far between, and otherwise it was a pretty uneventful trip down. The most fun was watching Bjorn swimming (or whatever you call what a bodiless head does underwater). I don't think that helmet of chum had ever swum before in his unnaturally long life, and even with the magical kiss of the depths, it was pretty riotous watching him fighting and flubbering around.

Mon'Goro seemed to be just as bored as I was, though he was keeping his yap shut on account of holding his breath. He didn't seem no worse for wear neither, though it is hard to tell if someone is turning purple when they is purple to begin with. He was just doggy paddling with his feet and watching his DWoid (which, of course, still has reception even a few leagues unda-da-ocean). We was really getting deep now, and it started to get dark, so I popped on my suit's floodlights and illuminated our surroundings. The queen pointed toward a glow in the distance.

"The palace is just ahead of us; we will be there in another few minutes." She fell silent and looked around the surrounding areas. "I don't remember all these sunken battleships being here before."

"Yeah, these elfin ships ain't put together very well; they seem to break at the mere kiss of dragon's breath . . . I'm just guessing educated here, I mean, how would I know how those would get from up there to down here?" I cleared my throat and looked for a subject to change to. I found it pretty quickly as we finally came into view of the royal palace of King Fathom. It was an immense structure built entirely out of rainbow-colored corals and sparkly seashells. I was just finished marveling at the "architecture aquatica" when I noticed the ruckus in front of the castle. The front gates was all locked up, and surrounding them were a variety of armored mermaid-men on sea horses. It looked like they was keeping out a gaggle of photographers and polished-looking reporter types who was all flashing pictures and shouting questions. I noticed, though, that we wasn't going toward the fray no more but was slowly moving away from the front gates and going around the back way. This seemed fishy. Ha! That's a good one.

"Hey Queeny," I shouted through my suit's speakers system, "if'n the palace gates is over there, how come we is going over here?" She looked like a fish caught in my headlights, literally, because these high wattage bulbs in my floodlights really blasted a spotlight on her mug. I courteously turned them down. She just flipped her hair and laughed a little girl's laugh at me.

"Silly captain, we can't can go through the front gates, there are too many paparazzi there, we would attract too much attention." Both

Mongo and I looked at each other as this girl seemed to love all of that razzle-dazzle. We wormed our way through some trenches and crags, and just as I was just about to say something, we found ourselves in a vestigial vestibule just below the castle. It looked like some old structure that hadn't been tended to in a while. The only thing in good repair was a group of menacing-looking mermaid-men that were guarding a thick, rust-crusted door. They seemed pretty surprised to see us—well, more specifically, to see the queen. They crossed their spears in front of the door and stood stoically as we approached. As soon as we got within thirty feet or so, one of the larger guards, a bristly whiskered bloke with tusks jutting outta his mustache, spoke up.

"Halt, Queen Sireen! You are forbidden to enter the castle by royal decree of King Fathom!" said the burly-looking guard in a formidable voice.

The queen got all slinky and started purring like a catfish. "Tut-tut, Sergeant Tusk, is that anyway to talk to an . . . old friend?" she said with a wink.

Bjorn was getting a bit jealous, and I admit I was getting a little tired of all these backdoor barricades and sideways shenanigans, so I plowed forward and greeted them with my customary courteousness. "Look here, Sergeant Tooths, I have a reward, sorry, *two* rewards to collect for bringing back your queen here! Let the woman enter so I can get my coin and get going away from this place," I said as I looked around for any sign of Fathom. If'n he lived there, he could be anywhere, and I didn't want to get caught on the wrong side of his new trident.

The queen seemed unfazed and walked right up to the guards with Bjorny frothing at her side. "You see that, my little warrior? They are trying to keep us from my welcome home party," she said, lovingly petting him on his helm. Bjorn was raging pretty hard at these dudes trying to flex on "his" woman.

"Let queen in silly pink castle or Bjorn smash you!" Bjorn said angrily, floating in front of the seven-foot-tall guardsman. Tusk and the rest laughed merrily at Bjorn, who was trying his best to stay rightside up. Unfortunately, they laughed at exactly the wrong time. Well,

Grimbeard Goes Fishing

laughing at Bjorn at any time, day, noon, or night, is the wrong time. With a roar of bubbles, Bjorn catapulted into the group of guardsmen with the force of a cannon ball. He took a bunch of spears to his dome, but since they were made of shells, mother-of-pearl, and other dainty material, they clattered uselessly off the steel helm that is Bjorn's head. In a few moments, the whole heap of them was stretched out unconscious-like. I knew they was just KOed and not dead, as when fishes die they does that weird upside-down floaty thing. Bjorn noticed this too, and he was about to delivers the "koodie-gra" by smashing a giant chunk of pink column on Sergeant Tusk's whiskered teefers, but the queen quickly intervened.

"You defeated the guardsman soundly, my little champion, but let's not escalate this little miscommunication to the next level; Sergeant Tusk still has his uses," she drawled on languidly. Instead of making fish paste, Bjorn used the pillar chunk to smash in the door what was blocking us. It was timed perfectly, as Mongo was just filching the key from around Tusk's neck. Shaking his head, Mon'Goro exhaled and covered his mouth quickly when he saw the air bubbles go a' bubbling out. Ol' Mongo can sure hold his breath, can't he? So with our path clear—aside from broken door, column, and guardsmen—we entered the castle.

NO MAID'S LAND

I would expect the castle and estate of the dang "king of the seas" to look a little more presentable, but it all looks kinda dilapidated and dusty. Or should I say "sandy"? Can you get dust unda-da-ocean? I runs a finger over a table and holds up a digit full of muck and sand. "Your maid busy or just taking a little vacation?" I said with my normal blend of humor and snarl. The queen came down the hallway with a look of disdain on her face.

"Oh, she has been getting busy, but the vacation is almost over for her. Come now, let us find the palace's dining hall, I am sure that is where my surprise party is being held."

Bjorn chimed in, all amiably, "Bjorn return queen to party and we can announce our love to all gathered!" He puffed out his invisible chest with maximum braggadocio. She picked up Bjorn and started canoodling him . . . It is not a pleasant thing to experience, so I'll saves you them mental images and speeds things up a bit. So we wandered and was having some difficulty with the random guard patrols we had to scuffle with. Well, after a few more scuffles and scrapes, we hit an area of the palace that was all dolled-up and shining. There was a bunch of tables set up and a whole mess of mer-kin servants, who was now fish-eyed at the queen as she entered the room.

"Where is that fool of a king?" she demanded regally. The servers all pointed their flippers and fins to a grand set of double doors. The queen went to the double doors and listened for a bit, all sneakily-like.

"Are you ready, my little Bjorny, to join the party?" she asked, all sinisterly. Bjorn bounced something fierce, causing some dude, an usher by the looks of him, to pop his head out from the other side of the double doors. "Shhh, will you! The king is getting ma—" was all he got out before the queen brained him a good one with a flip of her tail. She grabbed the double doors and just as she threw them open, I heard some fancy-accented bloke droning on and on, all theatrically.

"If any fish, amphibian, reptile, or half-and-half combination of the aforementioned here can show cause . . ."

Whoa, wait a minute. I knew them there words from somewhere, and all at once the whole thing hit me. Well, the whole thing hit me *secondly* because the thing that hit me *firstly* was the smell of a thousand different fishes, all gathered together in one enclosed room. Talk about a stank tank! So this second thing that my mind was putting together was what the queen was griping about after she read Mon'Goro's tabloid: "Separates" . . . "finds new love" . . . and all that points to one thing. Unfortunately this all came to me a few moments too late because the fish speaking orator-ily finishes up the second before my mind put them pieces together.

"If any can speak as to why these two people should not be joined in holy matrimony, speak now or forever hold your peace."

And that is when our girl made her play.

RUPTURED NUPTIALS

"Stop this immediately! This fornicating fishmonger is still married to me!" Queen Sireen screamed with a flourish.

Everyone turned and looked at us and gives a loud "OOHHHHH." I couldn't blame them neither as my swimmin' suit is quite badass and they probably don't get much chance to see such works of wonder like this unda-da-ocean. And, just as all eyes were on us from the moment we entered, they immediately turned around to the other end of the room to where a couple was standing, all polished and prettied up. The first half of the couple was a real fugly looking mer-hag and the other half was none other than the lord of the seas, King Fathom himself, and he had the expression of someone who is surprised, guilty, and furious all at once. I bet my illustrator won't even try to capture the look, he'll just do some back shot or have King Fathom's trident blocking his face. Watch, you'll see.

Anyway, the King went from looking at the queen to looking at me. I was feeling a little overdressed for this occasion, so I figured I'd just jump past the "how you doings" and "I like your new trident" small talk and get to my reasons for us crashing his wedding.

"So here ya go, King. I brought back your queen to her 'welcome home' party, and I think I'll just be taking off as soon as I can collects that million-dollar reward for your queen's, uhh, your old queen's return." The whole audience turned their eyes back to me and gasped in unison with a large "whoa." How do fish gasp anyway, don't they gets water down the wrong pipe if they do that? And now what is up with Queen Sireen? You'd think she'd be happy, what with me bringing her back and all, but she was just eyeballing me like I just called her something mean or derogatory.

"I am not old, you scruffy-looking sea-goat! I am the perfect age for a queen, and I am just starting to ripen," she said, composing her hair with an air.

"Starting to ripen? More like starting to ferment. Anyway, what's this have to do with my reward money?"

King Fathom started walking . . . swimming? Flapping, that's it. King Fathom started flapping his fins over and got real close to me and Sireen.

"How dare you show your face in my castle!" he said all imperialistically, and I weren't sure if he were talking to me or to Sireen. I was

about to reiterate my intentions of collecting the reward money for the queen's rescue (and return) when Sireen chimed in and escalated this debacle from a low grumble to an audible growl.

"How can you do this to me? And with the maid?" All the audience whirled their peepers to the other end of the stage to looks at the mer-hag bride-to-be. She just squatted there and raised a tentacle . . . to cover her belch. Eww, I think she inked a bit as well, and maybe the king smelled it, because he started stuttering on the words he was trying to scream.

"You—you have been gone for six months! You left me! You have been on the cover of every nautical newspaper, hanging out, literally and figuratively, with various scampis and urchins! You follow bands around like some grouper and are always dancing at striper joints and you try to blame me for your indiscretions?" said the king furiously.

"Whoooa," howled the audience. It was getting right hot in here! The king's eyes locked on me, and he switched the daggers he was using to stare at the queen and started throwing them at me.

"And you! You have the nerve to show that barnacled beard around my palace after what you have done? First you steal my trident! Then you de-scale my sister in the bait shack! And now you expect me to pay you for returning my soon-to-be-ex queen to me?"

"Booo! Booo!" howled the audience. I didn't think a fine upstanding dwarf as myself deserved such verbal insubordination, especially from this dang "audience." As a gentle-dwarf and guest, I swallowed the bit of bile that was building up in my throat and spoke with the grace suitable of this rabble of royalty I was surrounded by.

"All right already, I said I was sorry for your sister . . . Oh hey, how you doing, Neptuna?" I said as I saw the king's sister up at the front of the aisle. "Anyway," I said, turning back to Fathom, "all I needs is the million-clam reward for returning this here queen and the other reward for my previous bout of heroics when I rescued her from a bunch of shark m—"

"There is no reward! She just had you bring her back so she could crash the wedding! I am having the marriage to Sireen annulled and am now getting married to Mertunda—" It was the king's turn to get interrupted.

"Annulled?" screamed the queen. "You can't annul our marriage! It's been way too long for that, but do you know what I am going to do? I am going to divorce *you*!"

Just then the situation went from rancorous to downright danger-ous, as ol' Bjorn had finally had enough of his woman getting grilled in front of him.

"Go ahead and divorce; Bjorn, marry Queen Sireen!" he said, spitting the words at Fathom. "Drop the Nemo [clown fish] and get the hero!" (Sorry, had to switch that, you know, what with some people being litigious and all.) Fathom hooked Bjorn with a tine on his trident and lifted him to face level.

"Are you talking to me you . . . you . . . what in the blue hell are you anyway?" he said mockingly with a laugh, to which Bjorn replied as best he could with his standard answer: a well-placed helmet-butt that knocked the king's crown off his head, said crown surprisingly landing comically on Bjorn's helmet! I told you earlier how bad it is to laugh at Bjorn.

"Bjorn Huge is king of boring blue lands! All bow to new king!" The audience cheered and hooted and hollered; they was getting quite a show! Fathom shook it off and screamed for his guards.

"Gather this lot of land-scum and have them thrown in the dun-geons!" screamed Fathom. I saw this situation was desperate so I tried something I don't normally like to do. I reached into my suit's awesome storage containers and pulled out an old trident. Yep, you guessed it, Fathom's old bet he couldn't pay for.

"Seeing as there is a miscommunication, maybe you can just give me my millions, and in return—free of charge—I'll give you back this here old salad fork. It's a little bent and probably has some burnt plop-dogs on it, so no hard feelings," I said, extending the slightly bent tri-dent to Fathom.

Just then a member of the wedding party shouted out, "The hairy one drew a weapon on the king!"

And the whole room went ballistic. Members of the audience were diving left and right, and more and more of the king's royal guards came storming in. Queen Sireen charged at Mertunda, singing like a siren. Oh, hey! I get it now, Queen *Sireen*! It's like *siren*, but with one extra *e*. Oh, that is really clever! Anyway, it's probably more apt to say she was wailing like a banshee, what with all the colorful dialogue she was using. I will edit it so as not to offend those delicate dandies that gets offended by words and thinks I am speaking directly to them.

"How dare you seduce my husband, you [charming, mature female]!" she said as she went for the hair of the mer-hag. Mertunda just did a belch and sauced the queen in a cloud of purple ink. Speaking of purple, where in Bor's bloody bucket was Mon'Goro? I sure could have used his battle prowess, what with us against the king and his whole castle guard. I was dodging spiraling nets and barbed harpoons, and I even dodged Bjorn and Fathom, who were rolling around playing a game of "That's My Crown." I finally saw the hulking silhouette of the grape ape over to the side, watching his DWoid while deftly dodging and parrying the infinitely out-skilled guardsmen. Nothing distracts Mongo when he is watching his shows. His shows . . . what was the name of that one again? A light went on in my head—well not really, someone just bumped my suit and sent the floodlights shining right in my face. I dimmed the switch and started groping my suit's storage compartments for my DWoid, but I was coming up dry. I needed my DWoid, now! I looked to Mongo and shouted at him.

"Mongo, I need your DWoid."

Mongo gently shook his head and gestured to his eyes and then back to his DWoid. I made a lunge for it, but Mongo parried me just like he did with the guardsmen and I got right bent. Not bent at Mongo, but bent over physically, as five castle guards grabbed me and tried to pin me down. I didn't have time to deal with their fish tricks, so I blasted them off of me by expelling a few buffets of air from my suit's air tanks, which sent them somersaulting away. (I couldn't be doing that much more, as the tanks was reading about a half empty.) I noticed, with all the guards in the room with us, there was nobody watching the front doors, and all the paparazzi and reporter-types came streaming in, followed by all the cameras and boom-dudes. Flashes were going off and reporters was shouting and filming. The whole predicament was about ready to implode if something wasn't done immediately. I reached into my suit's compartments, and the roar of a gigantic croctopuss split the sea-air, and everyone stopped, dropped, and took cover.

"RRLLLAAAAAAAAAAAAAAAARRRRGHHHH!"

Bjorn and King Fathom ducked, in tandem, behind a toppled table and peeked out together. It would have been cute, too, if they wasn't all blackened, dented, and blued up with bruises. Queen Sireen was hamming it up in front of all the paparazzi and cameras and fainted into the arms, uhh, flippers, of a hunky-looking mer-kin. I saw a waiter with a tray of crispy-battered appetizers, and I politely yanks the tray away and addressed Mon'Goro.

"Hey Mon'Goro, want some fish sticks?" I said all temptingly. He just frowned disgustedly, shaking his head. I shook my head too, chuckling to myself. "No, Mongo, I didn't say fish—"

"RRLLLAAAAAAAARRRRGHHHH!" went the croctopuss again!

"No, I said fish sticks, fish *sticks*, not the, well, not that other thing." Oh, and for the slow-witted or those who don't have the humor of a six-year-old, say *fish sticks* fast, and then you are getting why Mon'Goro might not want to eat that particular treat.

I reached over and turned down my suit's speakers. My suit can communicate in all forms of sea-speak. That was croctopuss for "Hi." I saw everyone was still scampered away except for me and Mongo, and I turned back to the purple one, who had his earbuds in so he probably didn't hear my sonic subterfuge. Not that he would run from a croctopuss either, well, not just one; maybe three would do the trick.

"What do you say? They is still sort of crunchy," I say, poking them lightly. He readily shook his head "yes" just as I shook mine "no," much to his confusion. I pointed at the DWoid in his hand and then to the fish sti—let's just say "fish cakes," okay? He looked at me, defeated; he knows he is the better battler, but I am better at strategery. We made an honest trade, and I suddenly felt like I was being surrounded, probably because I was. I looked around, and a whole school of fish-men were looming in menacingly, harpoons glinting and nets whirling. Fathom had Bjorn in a helmet-lock, and things are looking pretty dire. It would be a huge battle, but luckily I don't need to always rely on fighting to solve things, and just like with Mon'Goro, whatever situation my mitts can't get me out of, my wits can. I turned to Sireen and Fathom.

"Stop now! This is no way for you two to behave! You are royalty, for Bor's sake! Start acting like it!" The crowd murmured and murgled something in fish babble, the likes of "Yah, the handsome one is right!" I pleaded to them using my best used-hovercar salesman's voice. "You two are the jewels of this here unda-da-ocean empire. We don't want to see some nasty court case bubble up over some simple misunderstandings, do we?" Sireen and Fathom looked venomously at each other, and just as they is about to go into round two, I spoke to them both with a language they can understand.

"You know, if you go to court, all those shark-smiling, snake-faced, bottom-feeding lawyers will get all the money, and you won't be left with two shells to play mancala with." To add emphasis, I pointed to a group of sharks, as well as a few snakes, a sea cucumber, and a starfish or two. They just smiled lecherously, adjusted their fancy ties, and started talking on their shellPhones.

I put my arms around Fathom and Sireen.

"You guys can't drag this through the muck, sand, or dust. If you are insisting on having an amicable separation, you should do it as a king and a queen should do it. Show a dash of class and an ounce of aplomb. No lawyers, no courts, just you two . . . and millions of viewers." I clicked Mon'Goro's DWoid on projector mode and beamed the screen on the castle wall. The whole room was greeted with an upbeat theme song while a very toothy eel, in suit and giant blond pompadour, greeted his audience and said, "Welcome to the . . ."

"Oh no," said the king as he holds his gurgling stomach.

"Oh yes," said Queen Sireen . . . and Mon'Goro.

THE MORAY SHOW

Everything happened so fast, what with all the cameramen and paparazzi around. All sorts of unda-da-ocean craft roared in, and those inside got to work erecting lighting and a stage. It took all of twenty seconds, it seemed, and then, in a slick, black stretch submarine, out came the man himself, Moray Pufferfish (that's the host's full name). I blinked, and next thing I knew the banquet hall had cleared, and the audience, wedding guests and reporters alike, was all filing in to take their chairs. I was surprised to see this actually worked! If'n I was smart, I would have just forsooked the double rewards owed to me by the queen, grabbed my crew, and got the blazes outta the place. But Bjorn still wouldn't leave the queen's side and Mongo got himself a prime spot, front row center, in an area labeled the "splatter zone." I was just about to "captain-up" and order them insubordinates back to the *Ol' Girl*, when suddenly the lights dimmed, and the crowd cheered. Well, I thought, I guess I could hang around till the first commercial break, which, of course, turned out to be a ha-yuuuuuge mistake!

"Hello and welcome to the Moray show. I am your host, Moray Pufferfish!"

The crowd went wild, and Moray ate it up by the mouthful. He turned from the crowd to a nearby cameraman and went into his soliloquies. "We all go into marriage with love and joy in our hearts. We look forward to building a life together, growing old together. But today we have a tragic tale of love that is floundering, struggling to keep its head below water. Today on the Moray Show, we would like to bring out someone who is a husband, a father, and even a king! Please help me welcome King Fathom." The audience cheered as the king took his seat next to Moray. "How are you today, King Fathom?" The king looked a little nervous, and if he had ever seen one of these shows, he should've been. Maybe that is why he brought his trident—well, his "newer" trident—I still have his old one, as he never took it when I offered it to him before the show.

"I'm not so good, Moray. I am married to an adulterous wife who leaves me for months at a time. I take care of her kids, pay her bills, bail her out of jail, you name it. I am done living my life like that. I found a new woman that I am in love with, and I intend to marry her!"

The crowd went wild for the king, and Moray, ever the maestro, conducted them all beautifully to a deafening roar before he silenced them with a waving-down motion of his tail.

"Well, it seems like you have some pretty strong words for your queen, King Fathom. What do you say we bring her out so she can engage in a polite dialogue with you? Ladies and gentle-fish, please give a warm welcome to Queen Sireen!" The room was immediately filled up with boos and hisses as Queen Sireen came storming out and launched into a not-so-polite shouting match with the audience saying that they did not know her, and if they wanted to say something, say it to her face. Several took the bait and swam down, only to be netted moments before the confrontation by some burly television security-guard types. The queen then went into an assault on King Fathom, verbally lambasting him with a tirade of abuse.

"You don't own me! You don't control what I do. I'm grown and I'm gonna do what I want to do!" Unshaken, the king of the seas "rose" up. (I don't know what you call it when fishes stand.)

"If you want to live your life singing songs and getting knocked up by all sorts of unmentionables and waking up on random docks, well, you should have thought of that before you put that ring on your finger!" Sireen was about to retort when Moray jumped in real slickery like.

"Now hold on, King Fathom, are you saying that Queen Sireen here is pregnant and that the tadpole is not yours?" The king spat more than laughed.

"She is always knocked up, but never by me." The audience gave a loud "ooooooh," to which the queen promptly told them to go "mate" with themselves. I was trying to hold Bjorn back but was having a difficult time of it. He was getting feisty and wanted to defend his woman's honor by smashing everyone out there that was against her. Luckily, the TV people duded ol' Bjorny up—they gave him a tie—and so I grabbed the satin "leash" and held on while he was spinning around. I almost lost my grip when an odd group of bruisers bumped into me. They looked like a dang seafood buffet; there were crustaceans, mollusks, arthropods, bivalves, and even a pinniped-looking dude what reminded me a lot of a younger Sergeant Tusk. I was about to deal with them posthaste when Moray chimed in and made a surprise announcement.

"Well, it seems there are some huge accusations being brought upon the queen by her husband, so let's put this all to rest by going to our most popular segment of the show, 'Who's Your Daddy?'" Cheers erupted from the audience—even Mongo was going nuts—and the thugs what

mushed into me and Bjorn was hurried onto the stage with Moray welcoming them with open eels.

"Joining us on the stage, the royal princes!" The king looked shocked as they all came up to take chairs next to their momma.

"Good morning, losers. Who bailed you buffoons out of the royal prison?" exclaimed the king, to which the queen screamed and fussed furiously.

"How dare you speak to our children like that? And you dare lock up your own sons in jail! What kind of father are you?" Now the audience took its shots at the king, booing and jeering him. Even Bjorn got into it!

"Boo, King Fat Ham!"

The king shook his hand flippers at the audience, yelling back, "Do any of these miscreants look like my progeny? Am I part *clam*?" The king pointed down the line at the motley assortment of sons landing on one blubbery and toothy-looking kid. "Do I look like a walrus?"

"No, and you sure don't [edited for our younger audience] like one either!" shouted the queen, to which the audience whooped and cackled. Moray was ever the statesman, keeping any laughs or guffaws to hisself as he sat down between the king and queen.

"King Fathom, why would you lock your sons, your own flipper and blood, in prison? Isn't that just wrong?"

The king composed himself and cleared his throat.

"First off, Moray, these dolts are not of my lineage; I am 100 percent sure of it. Second, I didn't lock them up; the palace cops locked them up! It's always the same thing with these guys; they drink all day, get wasted, and then fight all night!" said the king.

I blinked away some specks of sentiment from my eyes; I hope one day to have such fine, upstanding sons like King Fathom does.

The queen was feeling sentimental too and spoke very passionately from her heart. "Well, Moray, I am 1,000 percent sure that Fathom is the father of our kids!" She then turned her words to King Fathom. "And you better start acting like a father, too! It is time for you to be a man and step up to the table!" The crowd seemed to have her back as they started yelling at the king.

"Step up, step up, step up!"

Moray, from out of nowheres, produced a handful of yeller envelopes and waved them in the air for all to see.

"Well, backstage our guests were kind enough to let us swab their gills for a DNA sample, and we now have the results!" The king dropped his head into his hand and looked like he was about to ink his pants—if he was wearing pants, that is. The queen was up and dancing in his face, taunting and berating him, much to the delight of the crowd and Mongo, who was dancing right along with her till the bouncers told him to sit down, which he politely did. The antics settled down once Moray opened up the envelopes and started his pronouncements.

"King Fathom, when it comes to Prince Squidard (that be the squidly looking one) . . . " Moray let it build up till the audience was in a froth. "You are *not* the father!"

King Fathom rose up and started strutting around the stage, even doing hip thrusts into the face of the indignant queen with a "take-that" kind of vibe. Moray let the dance routine go on for a bit before he held up his hand and read from envelope number two.

"King Fathom, when it comes to prince Crabraham, you are *not* the father."

Once again the king went into his gyrations in front of what was now a visibly distraught queen. This went on for a while and I will just fast-forwards ahead of the next three, yep *three*, "King Fathom, you are *not* the father" moments. On the last one, the queen barreled backstage and was followed by the cameramen and Moray himself! He was back there, speaking all gently to her about how it was "just a few accidents" and that it "could happen to anybody." She finally bucked up and came back to the stage to much booing, to which Moray politely told them to quiet down. Once everyone had been seated or netted, the show continued with the queen and her sons on one side of the stage, and the king and Moray on the other. In the center stage, I noticed a strange thing. The camera crew brought out five more chairs. I was trying to figure out who else was coming to this production when the host started in with his simping sympathetics.

"So what happens now, King Fathom? Obviously Queen Sireen is upset and sorry for what she has done, right?" The queen nodded and wiped the running mascara from her face.

"I'm so sorry, honey. I know I did you wrong; can you ever find it in your heart to forgive me? I love you so much."

"What?" exclaimed King Fathom, Bjorn, Mon'Goro, and I at the same time. The king chuckled and shook his green man-head.

"No way I am taking you back. You made your bed and have *lain* and lied in it far too many times. I will continue on with my new life and my new wife!" The king seemed very cocky at the moment, but he should have realized that he was about to get cocky-blocked. Moray smiled and congratulated the king on his up-and-coming nautical nuptials.

"That's right, cheers to you and your bride-to-be, Mertunda, is that right? How did you two meet, exactly?" The king smiled and relaxed a bit. Big mistake.

"Oh, well, I hired Mertunda from a maid service a few months after I married this one here, as she was never the domestic sort," he said waving his trident at the mascara-massacred Sireen. Moray smiled eel-vily.

"So you met Mertunda because you hired her? She was your maid? You are marrying your maid? How romantic." The king looked at Moray with a flat stare.

"No, Moray, I am marrying the woman I love." Moray nodded con-genially at the king and then turns to the audience.

"Okay, well why don't we bring out King Fathom's new love and our lovely future queen to the stage. Everyone, please welcome the maid who's got it made, Mertunda!"

THE NEW KID IN TOWN

The audience was a mixture of cheers, jeers, and screams as the mer-hag galumphed to the stage and squatted on chair number one of five in the center. Queen Sireen saw Mertunda, her one-time maid, and started swinging and flapping viciously. After they scrapped a bit, the security guards separated them, and Moray shimmied over to Mertunda and sat down next to her. She was all dolled-up with makeup and a sequined dress. Unfortunately, that really didn't help. I always feel bad for some people when they is all prettied up and still looks shellacious, I mean, this is the best they will ever look, and they *still* look like a wreck. They say ya can't polish a turd, but I guess you can roll it in sequins. Moray wasn't affected by the horror in high heels plopped next to him and spoke to her in an affable demeanor.

"So Mertunda, you were the king and queen's maid for many, many years, is that correct? What was it like living in the royal palace?" Mertunda belched out a series of gurgles that really could have used subtitles for the studio audience.

"I mostly clean the palace, cook the foods, and raise little princes, while queen off swimming with sharks and king sleep all alone. My son lives with me, too. He a bit older than princes, but they seem to play fine together, though they say he play too rough." Moray stood up, freeing the chair next to her and a light shone at the corner of the stage.

"That's right, you have a son! Well let's bring him on our show! Everyone please welcome . . ." Moray started looking at his cards, not finding what he was looking for. Finally he tossed the cards and, like all veterans of live television broadcasts, adapted and overcame like a pro. "Let's welcome the king's maid's son!" The audience started laughing at the kid who entered, as he ain't the most gallant-looking galoot. I felt a pang of sympathy for him, as most kids go through a weird-looking stage, but that soon turned to admiration as the gorky kid picked up one of the laughing audience members and tossed him into a pack of others. The security guards started to surround him, but Moray ushered him over to the chair between his mom and King Fathom, patted the kid on his green-haired head, and turned back to the interviewees.

"So tell me, guys, how did this romance blossom into full blown love? Were there long, loving gazes from across the royal palace? Was there a courting period and gifts of sea-daisies?"

The king scratched his head.

"Well, Moray, it really blossomed naturally, you know? The queen was always gone, you see and, well, the maid was always around cooking and cleaning and uh, and folding clothes . . . making the bed, in the bedroom. Well, it just sort of happened, Moray, you know?" Moray nodded, listening intently.

"So, because the queen was gone, and your maid was around . . . you fell in love? How lovely is that?" The audience made an *awwwwww* sound. I think they needed to add a "ful" after the *awww* part, and that about sums it up for me. But, Bor's boudoir, I can't blame the king too much. I mean, that situation ain't too far from gas-station pizza if you think about it, although GSP's much more palatable than the king's new queen. Mertunda turned to the king and started to tear up a bit.

"There is something I need to talk to you about. It is about little Warnold, my son. Or, should I say, it is about little Warnold, *our* son." The crowd exploded with all sorts of riotous shouting. Queen Sireen let out a shriek and charged both King Fathom *and* Mertunda. The princes piled up on Warnold, not that they had much chance, as he was able to hold them off using Squiddard and Crabraham as club and shield to batter the others.

"You despicable, mer-hag-humping, bottom-feeding philanderer!" shouted an infuriated Queen Sireen. "You disrespect me in my own home, with my own maid and our kids' nanny?" The king dodged the blows, mostly by hiding behind Mertunda.

"It's my home—you left it, remember! And they are *your* kids! Besides, Warnold isn't mine! I mean, look at him, he looks nothing like me!" exclaimed the king. By then, the security guards had put everyone back in their seats, all heavy breathing, when Moray sat down, straightening his tie.

"Well it seems like there has been a secret going on for a while now, my king. You have a child? With the maid, a woman who isn't your wife?" The king shook his head defiantly.

"No, Moray, I am 1,000 percent sure that Warnold isn't my son."

Just then the self-righteousness fell from Fathom's face as Moray brought out another envelope. "Well, why don't we find out and be 10,000 percent sure?" he said, and the audience started chanting.

"Moray, Moray, Moray!" He shushed them down and let the tension build before he read the results.

"King Fathom, when it comes to little Warnold . . . you *are* the father!"

The whole stage erupted in a cacophony of chaos; fists and flippers were flung, and chairs went flying this way and that way.

"You cheater!" screamed the queen at the king.

"You're the cheater!" screamed the king to the queen.

Moray did his best to calm people down, but it took the combined might of the entire security team to get everyone netted and sitted down. I have to say, I was enjoying the show! I was glad I decided to stick around and watch the festivities. Let me clarify that: I *was* glad. Had I known what was going to happen next, I think I would have made a swim for it at the start of the theme music.

THE CRAPS HIT THE CRADLE

After a much-needed commercial break, we saw the stage put back together and new chairs replace the ones that got turned into kindling. Moray addressed the guests on stage with a voice what's like a father speaking to his kids (most likely *not* his kids).

"Well, what happens now, King Fathom? What do you intend to do with Mertunda and your brand-new son?"

"Well, Moray, I am going to step up to the plate and be the best father I can be to little Warnold." With that, Fathom gave the kid a big hug, and the audience "ooooh-ed" and "ahhhh-ed" at the sight. The sobs of the queen could be heard over everything, and Moray turned to her. She was surrounded by her spawnlings.

"And Queen Sireen, what do you intend to do now? If you like, we can help you find the fathers of your five lovely babies; we have people that can help and—" Moray was stopped mid-sentence by the clank of helmet on stage flooring.

"Queen never have to worry, Bjorn Huge take care of queen and fatherless bastards," shouted Bjorn, as he hopped out onto stage. One of the sons, the walrus-looking one boringly named Walter, tried to stop Bjorn.

"You ain't my da—*ouch!*"

Bjorn answered with a soft head-butt. "New son, sit down! Daddy talking to mommy." Moray, ever the pro, rolled with it.

"So, Queen Sireen, this is your new lover? What a striking profile he has!" The queen just waved her hand and made sort of a "meh" sound. Moray turned to his new guest and greeted him warmly.

"So it is Bjorn, is it? Well, hello, Bjorn, and welcome to the show."

Bjorn nodded back, "It great to be here Moray, now world see what creep King Fat Ham is, and now Bjorn show all world how to be real king! Bjorn now king of unda-da-ocean!"

King Fathom didn't take kindly to being called a porky porcine. They met center stage, and they was just about to let helmet and trident strike, when Moray asked a shocking question.

"Now that you mention it, who will be heir to the throne? If something happens to you, King Fathom, who is the heir to your throne?"

Queen Sireen stood up, shouting. "The King has five heirs already, Moray! He raised them so they are his children!"

Moray shook his head sadly. "I am so sorry, Queen soon-to-be-plain Sireen, but the law states that the heir must be of the noble lineage of the king. Unfortunately, your little darlings are not from King Fathom's royal loins."

Mertunda chimed in, all happily, "Oooh, my little Warnold, you see? I told you you would be the king one day! We will be rich!"

I swears I saw her eyes turn into coins for a second. Unfortunately, Moray came in with a shocker that changed them gold doubloons into lead slugs.

"Now I know this might come as a shock to you Mertunda, but Warnold was sired outside the bonds of matrimony, and as such, he cannot be considered a legitimate heir to the throne. That probably doesn't matter to you though, as you love the King, not his money! I am sure it was totally unintentional that you got pregnant by your employer, who is also a married man and in a position of great power and influence." Moray said charmingly to the mer-hag. Moray turned from the guests and looked to the closest cameraman.

"Well, what a day! What a show! We found out that it doesn't matter if you are a king, a queen, or just an everyday common person like us; we are all looking for love and hoping to find happiness in its embrace. I'd like to bring out a special guest who helped make this show possible today, our favorite air-breather and the last living dwarf, above or unda-da-sea, Captain Grimbeard!" The audience cheered like crazy, some even taking video on their DWoid. The usher was pushing me out onto the stage, much to my protestations. I'm not really the sort of dwarf that likes attention. There was a series of boos and curses, but they wasn't coming from the audience, no sir, it was coming from the stage. Queen Sireen was directing all sorts of colorful things to my general vicinity.

"I never should have made you take me back home. You have been nothing but drama ever since you fell in love with me!"

King Fathom was shouting at me from the other side of the stage and seemed just as riled up. "This whole idea was yours and *nothing* good came of it! You are going to get what's coming to you."

I was starting to get a little nervous at the turning of the situation, but these shows always seems to wrap up everything in a nice little bow at the end, so I was sure all this would have a happy ending. Moray was trying to calm everyone down, on stage and off, but they just kept on keeping on with the tirades and I decided to lend him a flipper.

"ROOOOOOOOOOOOOOOOOAAAAAALLLLRPPPP!" went the ol' swimsuit-super-speaker systems. The audience quieted down but didn't scatter like last time. The only one who got spooked was Moray, and after I pulled him off of me, we got on with the show. I sat in one of the remaining two seats that were unoccupied and unbroken.

"So Captain Grimbeard, we at the Moray Show want to thank you for your help today in bringing these wonderful couples together and allowing them to have some closure in their often tumultuous relationships. As a way for us to thank you, we have decided to help you get some closure of your own." I scratched my head, not understanding the words that were coming out of his mouth.

"Only closure I need, Moray, is on getting my reward money for rescuing and bringing the queen back here. I believe we talked of that money, i.e. gems, gold coins, etc., as all recognizable denominations that the Bank of Grimbeard will honor and accept," I said, kinda winded-like. I looked down at my air gauge and saw I was getting in the danger-zone area of remaining breathing time. I needed to get the heck out of here but Moray was still rhapsodizing all wistfully at me.

"No, no, my good captain, I am not talking about financial closure. I am talking about something far more beautiful and innocent that has gone on too many years without being addressed." I looked at him like, well, I still didn't understands the words coming out of his mouth. Ever the pro, Moray picked up on this and went into a bit more details.

"Picture this: a rugged captain, a dilapidated bait shack, and a young, pretty-ish princess . . ." I was nodding and suddenly I gasped, not just because I was in dire need of oxygen, but I also because I got what Moray was getting at. Moray smiled and welcomed his last round of guests. "Everyone, please give a warm reception to the lovely-ish Princess Neptuna!"

GRIM TIDINGS

Things was getting hairy as Bor's beard! Here I was, running out of air, the king and queen both were out for my blood, and now Moray was dragging a one-time fling of mine out into the public eye! What kind of "gotcha" journalism was this? I was just about to express my feelings to Moray's face (care of my fists), when the princess started up with the small talk. I noticed she had a tough-looking adolescent with her with big-brawy flippers and a mug of whiskers that might even rival my glorious face-broom.

"It's so good to see you again, my little captain. I had such a fun time on our first date; I really thought we connected. You said you would call me but . . ." The audience let me know they didn't approve with a battery of shouts and four-letter words not fit for print in this fine book. I could have said that my DWoid didn't have reception down this far, but that would have been easily disputed, as everyone knows DWoids always gets reception. Moray snaked himself in between us and started poking his nostrils into the princess's and I's business.

"So who is this big little tyke sitting here?"

"This is my son, Grimothy, Moray; he is actually the reason I am here today. See, he never knew his father growing up, and I thought it was time that he finally met him." Neptuna laid her dainty flipper on my hand, and the audience and Moray all gasped. I was looking around for what made them do so, and I saw Mongo clapping and with tears in his eyes. Well, I guess Princess Neptuna saw that I wasn't understanding the words coming outta her mouth, so she got a bit more to the point. (I hates when wimmens acts all coy and demure. Just tells me what you are getting at. I am many great things, but I ain't no great mind reader.)

"Grimothy," said Neptuna with tears in her eyes, "I'd like you to meet your father, Captain Grimbeard." Just then, the whiskery kid lunges at me, and I barely had time to throw up my arms in defense when he wrapped me in a big ol' sea-bear hug!

"Daddy! Daddy! BLOOOOOOOOOOOOOOOOOOAAARG!" he said all cheerily. Well, that last part was him hitting my suit's speaker controls, which blasted out a very suggestive mating call in croctopuss-speak. Good thing there wasn't none around to hear it, as that could have been a messy situation. I managed to pry myself outta the kid's embrace, and after we untangled our whiskers, I tried to get a grip on this dire situation.

"Now, look here princess, we just, I mean, I only put it . . ." I said, as I saw Fathom fuming across the stage. He was twisting his trident menacingly, probably thinking about making a dwarf-kabob. Moray then proceeded to pull out a yeller envelope, much to the crowd's pleasure.

"Moray, Moray, Moray," they roared.

"We have DNA results to see if Captain Grimbeard is the father of little Grimothy," Moray shouted back to the crowd. I was in shock, as I don't remember giving any samples of nothing. To nobody.

"Hey, you slippery sea-snake, how did you get access to my D or my A?" I shouted all hostilely.

"Please, my good captain, after you combed out your beard backstage, there was enough beard hair and dandruff to choke a whale!" said the "host-with-the-most." Fathom was beside himself with fury and was seriously ready to talk to me with the pointy end of his pitchfork. He got all spitty up in my facemask.

"If Grimothy is your spawn, you will dwarf up and take care of your responsibilities! You will get married, you will get a job, you will . . ."

"Oooh, I want a summer wedding, with sea-roses and everyone dressed in white," exclaimed Princess Neptuna exuberantly. All this was happening so fast, and the king just wouldn't let up on his verbal demands.

"You'll make this right! I told you that if you ever put your grubby fingers on my sister . . ."

"I done already told you," I said in all truthfulness, "I never touched her with my fingers!" Just then the king lost it. He snarled and swung his trident, hitting me with the impact of a tidal wave and cracking my suit's helmet. Water started pouring in, air started leaking out, and damn it if my suit didn't start launching off another series of croctopuss mating calls.

"SLLLOOOOOOOOOOOOOOORRG!

GRRRRLLLOOOOOORP!"

And a final, "RRRROOOOQOOOOOOOLLLLRP!"

I started fumbling with my suit; I really needed to figure out a better place to puts the buttons for that thing! Huh, weird, the suit speakers wasn't even on. Whatever was making them mating calls wasn't coming from me!

Moray started reading off the results of the DNA test, but I got bigger fish to filet. Fathom was attacking me with his trident, Princess Neptuna was planning our wedding, little Grimothy was holding on to my leg talking about "going to the park," and I was drowning in my own helmet! I looked around desperately for help, and I heard the mocking taunts of Queen Sireen.

"You're getting your just desserts! You spurn me and then make a mockery of my wedding! Now it's time to kiss your beard goodbye!"

I thought about what she was saying and she had a point! I thought that the best way for me to say goodbye to all this nonsense was to "kiss" it! I took a deep breath, sucking in as much air as was left in my mask, and with a few flips, I took it off and started swimming over to Queen Sireen, who was still jibbing at my predicament.

"Ah, so now you come trawling to me," she laughs. My eyes were bulging and my face was probably a shade of purple that could rival

Mongo's complexion. I didn't know if I could make it to her and also dodge tridents and might-be sons. Despite the interruption, Moray was still going on with the show that was already in progress.

"Captain Grimbeard, the results are in . . ."

"SLLLOOOOOOOOOOOOOORRG," went the croctopuss sound again; this time it shook the wall of the palace.

"When it comes to little Grimothy . . ." Moray let the suspense build up, and the audience was squealing in anticipation.

"GRRRRLLLLOOOOOORP," came another call, this one cracking the ceiling a bit.

"Captain Grimbeard you ARGHHH—" Moray never got to finish his verdict, as a bunch of ceiling came raining down on him like, oh, looked to be about a half-ton of bricks.

"RRRROOOOOOOOOOOOOOLLLLRP!" came the last call, and this one literally brought down the roof of the place, as not one, nor two, but three massive male croctopusses—croctopi? I still ain't never figured that out yet—opened up the whole roof, looking for the female croctopussy who was talking all nasty to them. I really wasn't able to take in all the commotion, as I was still making my way to Queen Sireen. Bjorn was encouraging me, thinking it was some sort of game, and I saw he still had his fancy tie on. I reached out, nabbed it, and pulled me up closer to him and Sireen. I was seeing stars, and a wave of black started blotting out them twinkles. The last thing I saw was the mocking red lips of Sireen, which is good, as they was exactly what I needed to get me out of here!

"Good swim, Captain! You need more exercise. I can . . . Hey, get beard off my woman!" he screamed, as I planted a big ol' kiss on Queen Sireen, much to both their surprise. She squirmed at first, but then seemed to get into it, a bit too much for my tastes. It was specifically the taste that grossed me out: a combination of tartar sauce, broken dreams, and Bjorn Huge. Not necessarily the trinity of tastes I would consider my favorite, but let's be honest: I wasn't kissing her for pleasure; I was doing it for survival. Bjorn didn't approve much none either way!

"Why you smooching Bjorn Huge's woman!" he demanded, in between head butting my knee caps.

"Hey buddy, I—*ooph*; I just needed—*ah*." Bah, it wouldn't do no good explaining that I needed her "kiss of the depths" (like what he got earlier in the story) to keep my lungs from exploding. He just saw a rugged, good-looking dwarf laying whiskers to his woman. I'd make it up to him later, and even though breathing weren't a problem no more, I still had an almost-full-house that I was dealing with—an infuriated king, a love-struck queen, and a jackass of an Assistant to the Captain, all fighting to get their mitts on me. And if that wasn't enough, I had a summer wedding to cancel, a probable paternity suit to clear up, and three ornery croctopi that was right pissed that they got their tentacles all up in a curl for nothing. That's okay. As you know, I always has an ace up my sleeve—or should I say "sneeze"?

12

A LOAD OF CROCTOPUSS!

King Fathom raised his trident high in the ocean-air and spoke in a tongue much like the croctopi. "KLLORRG AAALLLLGH DWWWOORG!" which my suit promptly translated back as *kill the dwarf*! I think his accent was messed up a bit, as only one of the three came a'thrashing at me. The other two promptly set about attacking the castle, the guardsmen, the guests, you name it. They basically went after everything that wasn't a dwarf. Seems my luck was turning from horrible to just plain awful. I managed to shake the queen free from my leg and worm outta a choke hold Bjorn somehow had me in. I saw Mongo charging up to help what I thought was me, but instead he went to the pile of rubble that was strewn upon the host of this here program. I saw him bring up Moray, who was still a bit out of sorts, only to drop him back down and hold up the envelope. I kindly asked my chef if he could lend me a hand.

"Look here, you purple-headed son of a second-rate sous-chef, help gets me out of this jam! Use your demon sword to cut a swath through this rabble," I said, as the king and his palace guards was surrounding me. Oh, and the one croctopuss what was understanding the words coming out of the king's mouth was barreling down on me from above. Mon'Goro nimbly fumbled into the envelope for the papers inside.

"I must first find out the gut-wrenching conclusion to this most dramatic saga that is unfolding in front of our very eyes!"

King Fathom and the guards came at me, and I used Bjorn, with his fancy tie, as a flail to keep them at bay. If something didn't happen quickly, I would be a rotisserie on King Fathom's fork! I managed to dodge and clobber with Bjorn (when he weren't trying to head butt me for kissing his girlfriend), when Fathom struck me with his trident, puncturing my auxiliary air tank. *Bor's bloody beard!* I forgot I had a secondary air tank! Bah, that would have saved me all this drama with Bjorn as well as the twenty bottles of mouthwash it eventually took to get rid of Sireen's smooch. Well, all that ran though my head about one second before I started shooting around the palace room. The air jutting out of my tank made me zoom around like a dang unda-da-ocean rocket, and it propelled me (and Bjorny) around the whole mess. I steered as best I could, me not being a certified unda-da-ocean-rocket captain, but I still did pretty well. I aimed at Mongo and made a grab, not at him but at the dang paperwork he was so interested in.

"Follow me to the surface, Mongo, and we can reads the results together!" I grabbed the envelope and that just plumb pissed him off! If this worked, I could take that H_2O-powered rocket straight up to the surface and leave this blue hell behind me for good! I saw Mongo hot on my flippered heels, screaming that he must "know the conclusion of this beautiful drama that has—" My attention was interrupted by a sputtering sound, and I noticed the velocity at which I was traveling slowing drastically. I looked at my gauges and saw the air left in my secondary tanks almost depleted. It also didn't help that I got all this newly added weight on account of Mon'Goro; he caught up with us and was climbing up to me using Bjorn and his tie as a rope ladder. I saw behind Mon'Goro that King Fathom (yelling about giving back his something-or-other), Queen Sireen, Princess Neptuna, Mertunda, and all their various bastard sons was swimming after me, followed closely by the palace guards, the audience, and even Moray and the other two croctopi! There ain't no way I was getting outta there, running on these quickly depleting tank farts. I needed an extra burst of propulsion to realize this plan and saw it in the shape of a gaping croctopuss maw that was about ready to swallow me, Bjorn, and Mongo whole. I steered into position—as I said, I am the best dang captain above or unda-da-sea. We blasted into the mouth of teeth, tentacles, and more teeth, and the beast chomped down on us. You would think that was the end of us, but I had planned for this exact situation. Just as the jaws dropped, I reached back and removed a certain something that caused the whole popping of the air tanks to begin with . . . King Fathom's trident! Can you imagine the luck? Well, I can, and as I says, "It takes hard work to make luck happen!" Since the air had done nearly depleted from my tanks, I couldn't think of a better way out of here than to take off on the inaugural flight of Air Croctopuss!

As you know, a lot of predatory fishes have very sensitive snouts and sniffers, and croctopi ain't different. I held on to the golden salad fork with one hand and shoved a mitt-ful of beardy goodness into this brute's sniffer. He started shaking his head and snorting, much to the dismay of his passengers (aka us). I tried again, this time letting go of the trident, and I shoved both my fists into the croctopuss's nostrils up to my elbows, one full of beard, the other full of Bjorn Huge, and the combined scents must be what done the trick. With a huge whoosh of air, snot, and passengers, the croctopuss sneezed with the force of a hurricane, knocking over all them fish types that was chasing us and unfortunately leveling what was left of the king's palace. I saw all this as we flew out of his mouth like human cannonballs (well, dwarf, beastling, and whatever-Bjorn-is cannonballs). We rocketed toward the surface pretty quickly but not quickly enough to forget how *dulllll* the middle part of the ocean is. After I woke from my nap (I always fall asleep when I fly), I saw that the ruined palace of King Fathom and Queen Sireen was nothing but an inky, blue blur far below us. When we got topside, I noticed that we was in the general vicinity of where we started, so I tried whistling for me ship, and in the distance, I saw the loyal silhouette of the *Ol' Girl* swoop into sight. She barked in happiness as we boarded her and proceeded to get cleaned up and dried off from all the croctopuss saliva, snot, and all-around grody-ness. I noticed

that it was nearing sunset, so I lowered my fishing boat into the water and hopped in. Mongo was holding on to Bjorn, who was still fuming at me. I tossed them the envelope, which I tucked safely in my beard.

"Don't you want to know the answer, Captain?" said Mon'Goro as he opened the envelope with much reverence. I shook my head happily.

"No thanks, I already knows the answer, but you go ahead, Mongo; I'd hate to be a spoiler!"

"You go fishing now? You have some 'splaining to do to Bjorn Huge!" Bjorn was still irate at me.

I waved and rowed out to open sea. "I'll explain everything when I come back, Bjorny." I proceeded to remove not only the old bent-up trident from the depths of my beard, but also a somewhat croc-snot-covered new one. "Sorry to rush off, but it is sunset and that is the best time to spearfish for croctopusses. I hear they got some real monsters out in these parts!"

EPILOGUE

Well, I finally sat down with Bjorn and explained to him I wasn't trying to wrangle up no affair with the queen; I was simply trying to get air. He sort of understood, and I made it up to him by promoting him from Assistant to the Captain to Assistant Captain. It is really just a title change with no extra duties or wage increasements. Unfortunately, he is still hung up on the siren Sireen. All day long he keeps searching the rocks and isles for his lost lady. That ain't the part that bugs me, though the worst part is he is constantly listening to the maudlin wailings—or should I say "whale-ings"—of that heifer, Adelf. Again, she is maybe a hundred pounds wet, so I don't know why I keep doing the fat jokes.

Mon'Goro finally opened the envelope after waiting all night for me to return. He wanted it to be perfect. Anyway, all his excitement crescendoed and then crash-endoed, when he found out that (I'm going to do this in my best Moray voice), "Captain Grimbeard, you are NOT the father." Hell, I coulda told him that, but like I said, I didn't want to give him no spoilers. Later on, after a follow-up episode, they found out that little Grimothy was actually the offspring of Sergeant Tusk, and they . . . Bor's beard, look what you made me do! I done made a spoiler! Well at least the part about Walter, the spawn of Queen Sireen and Sergeant Tusk, isn't . . . Damn it!

Well, speaking of the queen, she got her divorce, but ended up getting zilch, as she broke the terms of her pre-nautical nuptials that say that if'n she is unfaithful, she wouldn't see one clam! Turns out that really didn't matter, as she got a whale's weight in clams due to all the child support. Can you imagine how furious the king was, having to pay for all them galoots? Hey, I know they wasn't his, but the unda-da-ocean courts ruled that since he raised them as his own, he was responsible, as he was the only daddy they knows.

Mertunda and King Fathom never got married neither. She fell in love with and married Sergeant Tusk. She still got a payday though, as Fathom still had to pay child support for little Warnold, plus pay up on all the back support he owed the state, as she was receiving financial support the whole time! Funny thing is that the king is in charge of all state financials so she was doubling up! I know, what a racket. Well, all that money she got didn't stay in her purse too long, as Sergeant Tusk had to pay child support and back support for his and Princess Neptuna's kid, Grimothy. Since King Fathom found out his salacious sergeant was playing poke-the-poke with not only the queen, but also his sister, he fired him on the spot. And since ol' Tusk had no income coming in, social services went after his spouse—yep, Mertunda—and she got stuck paying the bill as she was married and was still working for the king, who kept her employed—otherwise his child support would go up! Can you believe the craziness? I am so glad to be a topsider, in the fresh, salty air, riding wave and cloud with the best dang crew a captain could asks for. I'd like to sings you a song before we go. Ahem . . .

I must confess, it's just a mess,
All of them troubles, down under the bubbles
I laughs at the notion, being unda-da-ocean,
So nice to be with my crew and me
Above the sea!

The End

ACKNOWLEDGMENTS

The Captain would like to offer the following scallywags
an extra share of grub, grog and 'gratulations:

To my Pops for teaching me drawing.

To my Grams for learning me cooking and manners.

To my Gramps for taking me fishing.

To the original crew of the Ol' Girl: Brother Ogre,
Brother Elf, Brother Micky Neilson (*New York Times*
best-selling blah-di-blah), and Brother Sea Dog.
Thanks for the inspiration for half the characters
and most of the predicaments dealt with in this
here collection of comedic catastrophes.

To the editorial tyrant, Cate Gary, for teaching me
English and helping spread the fine art of Grim-speak
to the linguistically challenged.

To the best dang spinners of stories there was,
is, or will be: Goscinny and
Uderzo, E.C. Segar, and the
inimitable Robert E. Howard.